The Complete Weird Epistles of Penelope Pettiweather, Ghost Hunter

JESSICA AMANDA SALMONSON is a recipient of the World Fantasy Award, ReaderCon Certificate, and Lambda Literary Award. Her previous books include *What Did Miss Darrington See?: Feminist Supernatural Stories of the 19th and 20th Century* from the Feminist Press at CUNY; two volumes of *Tales by Moonlight* from Tor Books; *The Encyclopedia of Amazons* from Paragon House, and Anchor Doubleday; *Anthony Shriek,* set in the streets of Seattle, from Dell Abyss Books, and the Centipede Press; *Amazons!* and *Amazons II* from DAW Books; *The Swordswoman* from Tor Books and the Science Fiction Book Club; *The Tomoe Gozen Saga* in three volumes from Ace Books, and Open Road Media; *The Death Sonnets* from Rainfall Books; and *Pets Given in Evidence of Old English Witchcraft and Other Bewitched Beings* from the Sidecar Preservation Society.

Her short stories have appeared in numerous anthologies in five languages, and in such collections as *The Deep Museum: Ghost Stories of a Melancholic* from Ash-Tree Press, and *A Silver Thread of Madness* from Ace Books. She has edited a number of single-author collections of supernatural tales such by the likes of Fitz-James O'Brien, Julian Hawthorne, Sarah Orne Jewett, Vincent O'Sullivan, Marjorie Bowen, Thomas Burke, Jerome K. Jerome, and many others.

She lives an anchoretic existence in a crumbling Edwardian home on a hilltop overlooking Puget Sound in the Pacific Northwest, with artist and potter Rhonda Boothe and some obnoxious but greatly beloved Chihuahuas.

The Complete Weird Epistles
of Penelope Pettiweather,
Ghost Hunter

Jessica Amanda Salmonson

The Alchemy Press

The Complete Epistles of Penelope Pettiweather, Ghost Hunter
© Jessica Amanda Salmonson 2016

Cover painting © Stephen Cooney 2016

Layouts by Peter Coleborn

This publication © The Alchemy Press 2016

First edition

ISBN 978-1-911034-03-2
All rights reserved

The moral rights of the author and illustrator have been asserted. All rights reserved.

No part of this publication may be reproduced, stored in a retrieval system, or transmitted, in any form or by any means without the permission of The Alchemy Press

All characters in this book are fictitious, and any resemblance to real persons is coincidental.

The Alchemy Press, Staffordshire, UK
www.alchemypress.co.uk

The Epistles

The Hounds of the Hearth	7
Serene Omen of Death in the Pike Place Market	31
The Spirit Shaman	41
The Forest in the Lake	47
The Oval Dragon	57
The Woman Who Turned to Soap	65
Legend of the White Eagle Saloon	73
Sarah, the Ghost of Georgetown Castle	83
Fritz, the Gentle Ghost of Shaw Island	89
Ogopogo	95
Harmless Ghosts	107
The Burnley School Ghost	117
The Queen Mum	133
Jeremiah	141
Notes on the Stories	163

Note: US English has been retained throughout this book.

Acknowledgements

"The Hounds of the Hearth", "Jeremiah" and "Harmless Ghosts" first appeared from Rosemary Pardoe's The Haunted Library, Psychic Sleuths #1, as a chapbook entitled *Harmless Ghosts* (1990) in an edition of 200 copies, twenty of which were hardbound by Tabula Rasa Press (1996). "Harmless Ghosts" additionally appeared in Robert Weinberg, S. Dziemianowics, and Martin H. Greenberg's *100 Ghastly Little Ghost Stories* (1993). "Jeremiah" additionally appeared in Richard Dalby's *Shivers for Christmas* (1995) and *The Mysterious Doom and Other Ghostly Tales of the Pacific Northwest* (1992). All three stories plus "The Queen Mum" were included in *The Deep Museum: Ghost Stories of a Melancholic* (2003) in an edition of 500 copies.

"The Forest in the Lake", "Serene Omen of Death in the Pike Place Market", "The Oval Dragon", "Legend of the White Eagle Saloon", "Sarah, the Ghost of Georgetown Castle", "Fritz, the Gentle Ghost of Shaw Island", "Ogopogo" and "The Queen Mum" all first appeared in *The Mysterious Doom and Other Ghostly Tales of the Pacific Northwest*. "The Queen Mum" also appeared in *Fantasy Macabre 15* (1992). "Legend of the White Eagle Saloon" additionally appeared in *The Seattle Times*, October 25, 1992, and in Mike Ashley's *The Giant Book of Myths and Legends* (1995).

"The Woman Who Turned to Soap" first appeared in *Phantom Waters: Legends of Rivers, Lakes and Shores* (1995), and was adapted as a three-person play performed at Washington State University's Wadleigh Little Theater in Pullman, Washington, February 13-15, 1996. It also appeared online in the Great Outdoors Recreation Pages.

"The Burnley School Ghost" and "The Spirit Shaman" were written especially for this present collection of the complete Penelope Pettiweather stories.

The Hounds of the Hearth

*"He that is unable to see the devil,
in whatever shape he is pleased to appear in,
he is not really qualified to live in this world."*
— Daniel Defoe, 1717

Theo Elliott sat in an easy chair reading from the pages of an old, leather-bound book when the lights went out. It was a usual occurrence, for the once-grand house was in ruinous shape and had needed rewiring for decades. He let the book fall flat upon his lap, sighed, and looked up with a resigned expression. The dying blaze of the fireplace reflected in his glasses.

He looked about the den, then turned his gaze upward, where the tops of bookshelves were lost in shadow. He stood, crossed the length of an oriental rug, put the old book back in its place, but turned swiftly when he heard an unaccountable sound.

It was only a snapping log in the fire.

He stood by the bookshelf and looked upward again. So many books! So many old, rare books! He'd lived in the house only a few months, his great-uncle having died with no other heir. Theo lacked the funds to repair the place. He often considered selling a percentage of the books, most of which were exceedingly valuable first editions from the previous two centuries, brought to America by an English ancestor.

Something always held him from the plan. As an introspective child, his one great dream had been to have a cavernous den such as this one, the walls all turned to shelves, the air thick with that certain odor of *book* which few but the most elderly librarians truly recalled. Books nowadays lacked the quality of leather and paper, the aging fineness. Even glue had become synthetic, odorless. There was nothing in the library that could be considered replaceable.

He couldn't sell the books. He couldn't alter the excellently oppressive atmosphere and mood of this glorious room.

On the other hand, he couldn't afford to fix the roof, rewire the electricity, and reinforce the foundation before the floors became even more warped and uneven. He would have to sell *something*.

The fire popped again, a sound like a snarl. The dim, orange light played weirdly about the room.

What a foolish dream it had been anyway, to have a den. Growing up, he'd never seen his uncle or his uncle's house and didn't have the vaguest idea where such a strange conceit could have originated. Children weren't generally obsessed with such things, were they?

The feeling intensified as he grew older, though he spent the majority of his thirty-seven years coming nowhere nearer his daydream of a book-filled den. He'd lived hand-to-mouth caring for an aging great-aunt, pursuing no course of his own. Then his aunty died with so many medical debts that her dingy two-bedroom coöp apartment had to be sold. Theo was on his own for the first time in his life, with only a tiny profit from the sale of the coöp. What was he going to do when the money ran out?

Fortune came as a strange, friendly force at times. He stumbled through his miserable life for more than a year. Then, when things seemed their most hopeless, an upstate attorney succeeded in tracking him down. Theo was informed that his great-aunt had had a brother. Really? She'd never mentioned him. Estranged, no doubt. The old uncle had died about seven months before, and Theo was the sole survivor of the Elliott family, therefore heir. Theo asked a stupid thing: Does the house have a den. Yes, said the attorney, the house had a den.

Theo moved upstate.

Even owning a house free-and-clear meant trouble. The taxes were two years in arrears; plus there were hefty inheritance taxes. There were attorney's fees to pay off a bit each month. The house itself had been let to ruin during the last twenty years of his great-uncle's eccentric life, and repair requirements were past the point of emergency.

But, well, Theo had his den at least, didn't he? His lifelong dream had come to fruition. It was eerie how much the den was like the one he'd longed for. But, despite the total realization of his wish, a dean wasn't the end-all of life, was it? It didn't mean a thing. A foolish, private, unpresumptuous dream had bolstered the dreariness of his wretched life. The dream had been taken away from his by its very realization.

Theo Elliott wasn't particularly happy.

And he would have to sell some books.

The fire flared, making it momentarily bright in the

room. The other rooms would be pitch-dark, however, and Theo had to think about going into the dank basement to check the fuse box.

He went to the expansive leather-topped desk and opened one of its myriad drawers. He scrounged through loose sheaves of his uncle's meandering, meaningless notes. "I should burn these old papers," thought Theo. "They're of no earthly use to anyone." He found the flashlight, which had somehow burrowed its way to the bottom of the drawer. He tested it, the batteries proving strong since he'd replaced them shortly after the last blackout in the house, when he'd been forced to fumble around with the dimmest of beams.

The fire burned high, which was surprising, as only moments before it had seemed to need more wood. He mustn't leave the den with the fire uncovered, so he approached the fireplace intending to pull the screen. He stopped some six feet from the hearth, however, and stared. The blaze had an extraordinary pair of shapes within it. He'd often watched the dancing devils which could be found in any fire, just as ghostly shapes can be picked out of clouds in the sky. But here the fiery shapes seemed so specific, so carefully *held.*

There were two slender hounds standing in the fireplace.

Well, they couldn't be hounds, could they? They were flames dancing upward in the shape of hounds, but still the effect was tremendous. They had black eyes—holes in the fire of their evil visages—and two pairs of especially pointed licks of flame for ears.

They were devilish animals of molten bronze, their

legs, their torsos, their long muzzles shining. Their fangs were inverted flames. That was odd; small flames perfect as from fresh-trimmed wicks, burning upside down from the muzzles of the hounds.

Why, that's quite extraordinary, thought Theo. I wonder how long the flames can stay like that?

There was no sense that the fire intended to break up into other shapes. Theo squatted down. He heard his knees crack. The fire itself was strangely quiet. He stared into the blaze, mesmerized by the weird beauty of the hounds.

Then the fire flared again. It seemed the hounds had leapt across the hearth! Theo started to stand, shouting but they bore him down. Their snarling was the sound of an inferno. They fastened to his neck and right arm. The flashlight went rolling. He choked out one more shout, then burning fangs tore out his vocal cords.

Theo Elliott felt nothing more. Shock, mercifully, took away his senses. It was three days before the attorney happened by on the matter of an overdue payment. The door was unlocked and he entered. The house was still. When he entered the den, he saw the charred remains of Theo Elliott, and gasped. Soon after, police were puzzling over the matter, for the remains were too cooked to have been moved without falling apart, yet it seemed impossible he'd burnt on the spot. The Oriental rug beneath the horrid corpse was not so much as singed.

The attorney paid the property taxes. He put a lien against the house, expecting it to fall, in time, into his own possession. He was that rarity of his profession, however; that is, he was an honest man. And so he decided to make one more concerted effort to locate some surviving member of the Elliott family.

My dear Cyril,

I found out about the above case through a mutual friend of the attorney. At first I knew no more about it than the police, except that I was less easily convinced that Theo had been cooked to the bone, then walked about the house until he was sufficiently cooled off to fall down somewhere, catching nothing else afire.

The hounds of the hearth were described in those notes which Theo fortunately never cleaned out of his great-uncle's expansive desk. But it was some while before I found the notes, and longer still before I could organize them. The old fellow, Durkin Elliott, apparently had a singular aversion to using a bound diary. Indeed, according to a neighbor, old Durkin had an unreasoning dread of books of any kind. In that was another mystery, considering the spectacular collection of old books in the elder Elliott's keeping.

There was plenty of research material here, I was certain. Quite likely I could find enough information for an entire chapter of my book *Northwest Houses and Their Ghosts*, out of print now but only an outline and a glimmer in my eye at the time.

I called upon the attorney. He was a balding, older, dignified fellow by the name of Jeremy Stone. I explained that our mutual friend, the retired Reverend Nicholas Vanikov, had told me about certain events — only that which was not privileged, naturally — and that I had already taken it upon myself to interview neighbors of the Elliott estate.

I asked if I might rent the house through the coming winter, both as a retreat where I might comfortably complete my book, and as an added subject of my studies.

Being a slight, middle-aged woman who dresses in a businesslike fashion makes me, perhaps, nondescript, but it has its advantages. I could be colorful like my colleague Mrs. Byrne-Hurliphant, but then I'd have her problem of always being dismissed as an utter crackpot by such conservative men as Mr. Stone. My amiable manner won him to my favor. Also, I'd already written four books in my specialty, and this gave me a certain glamor in his mind. People have such romantic notions about authors, as you, too, have no doubt encountered, Cyril! It still strikes me as odd, ordinary as I happen to be, that some people will insist on viewing me in a romantic light, when in fact a book or two is nothing at all. Mr. Stone had never seen one of my books and, chances are, did not know a soul in the world who owned a single edition. Nevertheless, he was impressed that I wrote books, and wanted to be of aid in my research, hoping no doubt for a brief nod in my Acknowledgements.

His eagerness was also born partly of his own misgivings about the estate — or, rather, about the death of the younger Elliott. The police had dropped the matter, having neither the imagination nor disposition to cope with what confronted them. But Stone had designs on the house, and enough conscience that guilt tweaked at him for taking advantage of a grisly situation. His small qualms would be alleviated by allowing me my intensive if, to him, peculiar investigation.

Mr. Stone did not believe in "ghosties and ghoulies" as he called them, but he was willing to let me poke around to heart's content. He said a winter house-sitter was an asset and he would not charge rent, trusting me to do no harm to the premises. The electricity was turned on at Mr. Stone's expense. I had to pay to get oil in the furnace. The house had been settling for ages, and a bit of the front door's underside needed shaving, and the lock needed to be lowered in the frame, before the door would open and close properly. Mr. Stone generously did this with his own tools. He also helped me unboard the main-floor windows.

Being somewhat a country setting, with the Cascade Mountains as backdrop, the house was the perfect environment to work on my book, entirely aside from the possibility of the added chapter. I brought my typewriter and my notes and settled in rather quickly. The first couple of days I nosed around here and there, getting no real work accomplished, getting used to the place. I sensed from the first that the house was unique and, yes, one way or another, I was bound to find useful data.

When I uncovered the elder Elliott's notes regarding the hounds, I can't tell you the extent of my excitement. You must realize how much of my work has indeed been speculative or from secondhand accounts. Even if I found nothing more than an old man's fantastic descriptions, it was a revelation. But as you also know, I am rather more honest than most about the verifiability of my material. I am always quite frank about what is hearsay and what I was personally able to witness. This is what puts me apart from Mrs. Byrne-Hurliphant, even if I must delineate the difference myself. Thus I was hoping to experience the phenomenon with my own eyes and senses, and so spent the majority of my working hours in the den, and keeping a steady fire.

There was unsplit wood in the back of the house, magnificently aged. I split so much that my poor spidery hands felt too arthritic to type much in the evenings. I stacked more than a cord, which would not have lasted long had it been my primary source of heat (and I dread telling you what I paid out in oil that winter) but I heated only the den with wood, and spent a good deal of time before the glow of the fireplace.

Early on, I figured out that Theo had been reading something the night he died (the minutest details of my opening scenario have, in fact, been verified to my satisfaction). You might be interested in my investigative process.

By the unbound diary notes of Durkin Elliott, I was able to learn, in his own words, the extent and nature of his phobia regarding books. He hadn't touched his own library in years. Thus, by finger marks in the dust, I was able to identify and classify every book Theo handled, removed, thumbed through, or read entirely.

The book he was reading the night of his demise had not been pushed entirely into its place, by which clue I deduced that a noise caused him to turn quickly, at the very moment of putting the book away.

He had been reading a first edition of Conan Doyle. It would spoil the seriousness of my narrative to tell you exactly which book, so I will leave that to your own Holmesian deductive prowess, while assuring you that your inevitable surmise is quite correct.

Most of the books in the library were of a macabre nature. Durkin's phobia was developed late in his life, perhaps because in his younger years he read rather too many of those books, and this wore at him when senility approached.

I was surprised to find such rarities as an 1802 edition of *Tales of Superstition and Chivalry* in as mint a condition as so old a book is ever found; and a set of rebound six-penny chapbook horrors from about the same period. There were the only copies I have ever seen of *Spectre of the Murdered Nun,* undated but I think about 1807; *The Factual Account of the Thirsty Woman of Tutbury Seen Wandering About Seven Years After Her Hurried Death* dated 1777; Percy's 1765 *Reliques;* and some fascinating oddities — perhaps the complete works — of one Anne Letitia Barbauld, including her 1773 treatise, *On the Pleasure Derived from Objects of Terror.* You would also be interested in a book called *Tales from the Convent,* to my knowledge hitherto unknown except in a passing reference to it in the preface of another of the same author's books, *The Bravo of Venice.* As a matter of fact, everything by M. G. Lewis seems to have been in that library, no edition later than 1836, most from about 1808.

Of this extensive collection I established that the younger Elliott definitely read *The Monk* in first edition; Hoffman's *Elixier des Teufels* in the original (Theo had his faults, but he did read French, Italian, German and Latin); an 1801 anthology called *Tales of Wonder;* a very carefully handled early 1600s hand-illuminated copy of Bouguet's *Discours des sorceriers;* the equally old *Decretalium Corpus Canonicum Glossatum;* and several French fantasies set in Baghdad and the like, some which I have never heard of previously, dating to about 1705 at the earliest, and clearly influenced by Golland's first volume of *Arabian Nights* which was translated from 1704 onward, and which were also in the library. The only other copies I've ever seen of one of Golland's books was in your own collection, and forgive me for letting you know that yours is in comparatively shoddy condition.

Well, after I had catalogued for future reference everything that Theo had read, I found myself reading some of those same old books. It was a rare opportunity, after al. Indeed, I could easily have spent my winter doing none of my work, preferring to read excellent copies of rare and even unknown gothics and terror tales. In fact, it just this moment occurred to me that I should enclose copies of my notes about *The Teeth of the Abbess* from 1711, and *The Terror from America* which purports to be a translation from the 1640 Italian, but so much like the English horror of the eighteenth century that I just suppose the translation bears little resemblance to the original. You may, of course, quote my notes freely in your fine little antiquarian journal, though of the present letter, I must beg you hold it in confidence.

This is somewhat off the topic, isn't it? Suffice to say Durkin's senile thinking might well instill in him a dread of the very things he found so fascinating when a heartier fellow. As the library was brought to America by Durkin's ancestor Charles Ingold Elliott, and had belonged before then to the very same London family, from a time when most of the books were new, it occurred to me that Durkin might never have wanted the books imposed upon him in the first place. But he seems to be the one responsible for adding things to the collection when he himself was a young man. There were first editions of Poe, Hawthorne and Brown. So we may safely assume his fears were developed late, and that the collection had not been kept unwillingly in the beginning. As for Theo, he seems to have inherited not only the property, but some genetic fascination for the subject matter in these veritable family heirlooms.

Theo had not lived in the house long enough to leave his own mark upon it. But he had brought with him some personal effects from which I was able to draw clues about his attitudes, likes and feelings. In a tattered cardboard box of odds and ends from his youth I uncovered some perfectly abysmal horror stories which he had penned. It was an interest he properly dropped while still a teenager, having small aptitude for composing fiction. Some of them had been harshly graded by teachers who didn't like them for content rather than style, but mostly it appears he never let the majority be read by anyone, which was just as well.

A recurrent image in these juvenile pieces was a library den. Sometimes it was haunted, other times inhabited a father-figure of the sort Theo lacked in real life; or his fictional den would at least contain an arcane tome which started the protagonist off on some weird adventure. I must suppose from this recurrent setting that poor Theo found his dream-come-true in the library den of his inheritance. I placed that very supposition in my opening reconstruction of Theo's last living experiences.

I sidetracked myself from telling you what Durkin

Elliot had to say about the hounds. He described them at length, though his scrawly penmanship was in places undecipherable and important details remained unclear. He often called the hounds "guardians" though he was vague about what it was they guarded. Your own mind is quicker than mine and I'm sure you're already gathering that the hounds were guardians of the books. It took me a while to work that out, and I still have questions about it. Yet, I will stand behind my hypothesis that Theo intended to break the collection up because of his financial woes. Certainly the Lewis volumes alone could have kept him in the black for years, ending his strife, if he could connect with a collector and dealer such as yourself — or even myself, supposing a wish could conjure funds.

The hounds would not stand for it, in any event.

Durkin had a theory as to when the hounds arrived in the house, which will take some historical backtracking to explain.

By your evaluation, living where you do, the mansion might not be impressively old. But for the Northwest corner of America, mid-Victorian architecture is quite antique. It's a remarkable house, really, though you might spurn the thought, rascal that you are. When it was built, great care was taken in bringing in the best skilled laborers.

An Irish immigrant was hired to build the chimneys. Charles Ingold Elliott was entirely cognizant of the fact that American masons were morons then as now, and American roofers somewhat worse. The fireplaces in this old house are truly remarkable, of an East European style as near as I can judge without actually seeing the interior ducts, and definitely the work of a most skilled Irish hand.

The books were at that time still in New Bedford a coast away. The patriarch Charles Elliott was already an old fellow when he uprooted his family again and brought them to the Northwest for the sake of lumber and shipping investments. He'd already realized the American dream of wealth, unlike most who came across the sea in his day; but at an advanced age he was still an adventurer, if it was a matter of profitability.

The Irish mason had been sorely mistreated in America, and this seems to have been his first opportunity at gainful employment. It seems to have been Charles' opinion that the Irishman should therefore express no end of gratitude. Partway through the labors, the poor mason had an emergency in his family and asked for an advance of payment, but crabby Charles refused to extend even one cent for work not completed. Demeaning himself before the patriarch served only to make the stingy fellow more stubborn.

The long and short of it is that the Irishman was pushed to the limit and there was a tussle. The old miser was nearly killed in his mostly completed den. Subsequently the mason was arrested, and hung himself in jail.

The third chimney was finished by another mason (it shows) and a forth never built at all. About the same time, a woman was found dead on the path to the house from the lane. Nobody knew who she was, but it doesn't take much to suppose she was some relative—wife or sister—of the Irish mason. She'd been seen lurking about the property a few days before she turned up dead of pneumonia. Perhaps her intention had originally been to ask for the dead mason's last day's pay. If so, she never worked up the nerve to announce herself, preferring to let herself die upon the path as a sort of protest against Charles Ingold Elliott's mischief.

Shortly after these events, the hounds began to appear in the den fireplace. Of all these matters, Durkin's account is mainly secondhand. I did discover Charles' own papers in a corner of the attic, but they were useful only in calculating the one-time wealth of the Elliotts, frittered away before Durkin's time.

Durkin drew from the family's oral accounts, and we may trust him to a degree. Of course, the books to which the hounds seem to have become attached were still in New Bedford, arriving shortly after, rather than before, the first fireplace phenomenon. Thus the connection between the hounds and the books is not entirely clear. You know enough about these matters to comprehend that otherworldly events are rarely quite pat enough to satisfy our own down-to-earth sensibilities.

I could find no documented evidence of the hounds causing trouble, though they were certainly unsettling, and most family members and guests came to avoid the den. There was always to be found one family member willing to care for the library, however — none so devotedly as Durkin.

As for the original patriarch, I seem to have established that he did die of burns. I fear I cannot provide evidence of unusual circumstances. The local town hall has records going back to the town's founding, but of the cause of Charles Ingold Elliott's death, it is synopsized in a single word: fire. He might have caught his pants ablaze while burning weeds for all I know. Durkin made no note of it whatsoever.

In time Durkin became an uncommunicative hermit, known to very few, though some of my information comes from an elderly woman who brought him fruit from time to time, and who still lives on an adjoining estate. After Durkin's parents died, he lived in solitude, though he did have siblings who owned a share of the house. My next avenue of investigation was, therefore, intended to uncover the reasons for lack of communication between his siblings and himself.

My perversely romantic nature would like to report a terrible incident causing the falling out, but it seems to have stemmed from entirely mundane feuds. It began when most of the siblings were already off on their own in other parts of the state or country. When their mother was dying, Durkin alone was there to care for her, having been bound in any event to the library and thus the only stay-at-home. After her death, his brother and two sisters did not wish to credit him any noble intentions. It was their wish to sell the house out from under him, dividing the inheritance equally.

The family's fortune had long been a thing of history, and there was a lot of squabbling about how the scraps would be shared. It was, moreover, a bad time in general for America, and it proved difficult to find a buyer for the mansion, far as it was from areas of modern commerce. It's also obvious that Durkin, as the caretaker of the estate, was in a good position to stymie any successful real estate transactions, and furthermore was simply unlikely to add his needed signature to those of his siblings. In time the house was taken off the market and the ill-feeling against Durkin was so extreme that he was to spend the next forty years of his life without any contact with the others. In the end, he outlived them all, having the last laugh indeed, though perhaps he had nothing to laugh about.

I did not see the hounds myself for the longest while, though I stoked the fire almost nightly, and did my work before that fated hearth. I spent perhaps too much time reading rather than working, and courted the notion of making an offer for a portion of the library, to go into debt for it if necessary, though I didn't know if Mr. Stone was in any position to consider an offer.

I imagined that I could obtain a loan sufficient to purchase the top twenty-percent of the library. Then I could impose upon yourself to find buyers for a few choice items, perhaps obtaining some of them for your own collection, allowing me to pay off my bank debt. In the end I'd be left with some of the finest volumes of the rarest books of their kind.

Such was my wishful design.

It was while pondering these greedy notions, and reading, I must tell you, Reverend Maturin's *The Fatal Revenge of the Family of Montorio*, that I saw the two hounds watching me. I must also tell you I was unnerved. Though this was far from my first encounter with the supernormal, yet was my heart inclined to miss a few ticks. Ordinarily I have been able to research a given phenomenon to my satisfaction and have a good beforehand knowledge of what I might face, thus minimizing fear and danger. In the present case there were too many puzzling aspects: Were the hounds really the doleful specters of two unjustly treated Irish immigrants? Why did they manifest themselves as hounds rather than, say, crows or cats or even their original human shapes? Why did they feel protective of a library which came to the house after the hounds themselves? What was more special about this fireplace as opposed to the other two the mason had put his hand to making, other than his having argued before this particular one?

Without greater awareness of their purpose, I could not be certain they would not do to me what they had done to poor Theo. Though they might not have done anything else suspicious in their decades of haunting that hearth, Durkin yet feared them, and Theo ought to have feared them more than he did.

In short, I was afraid.

But they did not leap across the hearth. They only watched me with their black eyes in their golden faces. They sat there amidst the burning logs comfortable as you please. Surely they were hating manifestations of something, so evil did they seem to me in both their physical aspect, and the chill they put on my inner sense.

I had my camera of course, with necessary lens attached, but it was not in hand. I crossed the carpet and took the camera from the desk. When I faced the fire again, the beasts were gone. I set the camera on a tripod before a well-stoked blaze and was totally prepared for their next manifestation. Then I took down a book from a shelf, quite at random. Only later did I recognize it as a relatively recent book, by that library's standards, and quite a worthless one if you ask me, entitled *The Outsider and Others*. I cleared my voice and proclaimed at my strident best, "Show yourselves, my fine doggies, or I shall toss this loathsome book into your mouthers."

Well, that's all it took. They were there quick as a blink, but stayed somewhat longer. I pressed the button and heard the shutter click. I wound forward and pressed again as I was saying, "Rather easy to tease, aren't you, my wondrous whippets? In reality I've no intention of harming your precious books at all." I laughed. I must confess it wasn't easy to address them in so cavalier a manner. It was quite like my first experience as a child, when I was confronted by some truly ghoulish figure, and remarked to them with a forced off-handedness, "I won't hurt you one bit unless you try to get me first." I've since found that specters of all kinds are rather easy to bluff past, the afterlife intellect being apparently simplified.

The dogs glowered in such a baleful way that I knew they hated me for having tricked them. They stayed until I had four pictures, three of which came out very well. You'll appreciate the attached print.

It would seem I had everything I needed for that hoped-for chapter! But, as you're one of the few individuals who know my books particularly well, you'll already have recalled there being no such chapter in that book. I was ultimately unable to include the photographs or the account of my findings, due mostly to deeply personal and troubling responses which I shall have to explain.

To one so jaded as I have become to events of this kind, who has lived her whole life with this inexplicable sensitivity to curious events of this world and the next, you may wonder what indeed could so horrify me that I have been unable to tell a living soul about it until this very private missive to a trusted friend. It may well be that to one such as myself, true horror takes on forms other than that for most people.

The winter was only half over, and I thought I had a few more weeks to reside in the old manor. But Mr. Stone arrived one evening to inform me that I would have to leave in only a couple of days. It seems he discovered a distant cousin to whom the house must be transferred. However, after several long-distance calls, Mr. Stone established that the heir had no interest in making a long trip. A few legal powers were being sent back and forth, but the gist of it was that Mr. Stone had power of attorney over the matter of liquidation, and would take a fat commission for his troubles.

The first things to go would be the furnishings. That was why I would soon find the house uncomfortable, Mr. Stone explained, devoid as it would be of chair, table, or bookshelf.

You are getting ahead of me, Cyril, I can tell. Yes indeed, when he was part of the way through his explanation and apology, Mr. Stone's face went suddenly ashen. We were in the den, of course; and I did not have to turn around to know what he was seeing in the fireplace.

At that moment, I said in a loud, theatrical tone, "But, of course, Mr. Stone, the books will remain in this room under any circumstance, am I right?" I winked at him absurdly, and fortunately he did not think I was flirting, but caught on to my charade with the kind of sudden awareness people often have in a genuine crisis. "Of course," he said. "Of course. Why on earth would the books be removed?"

I led Mr. Stone out of the room without once looking back. He was sweating and whispering banalities, until I said, "It's no good whispering in front of them. They can read our very thoughts while we are in their room." As we passed out of the chambers, I added, "In fact, our little charade probably only threw them off the scent for a few moments, long enough for us to get out of the library. I don't know if we were in danger, Mr. Stone, but I must tell you bluntly, I think we were."

"I know your specialization," he said shakily, "but you must forgive me having thought it merely a 'subject' and not a reality of any sort."

"No apologies required, Mr. Stone. I always lead people to believe it is merely a 'subject' that interests me, lest I scare them or, worse, have them think me daft and thus refuse me their cooperation. In any event, as you are now privileged to understand, there are things of this world that ought by rights to have gone on to another. I'm absolutely convinced the hounds burnt poor Theo Elliott just as you found him, and they did so because he planned to break up the library for financial reasons. I fear I can't tell you much more than that about it. But right this minute, I wouldn't go back into that room. When the fire has gone out, it shall be perfectly safe, but not until. I wouldn't recommend ever starting another fire in there, either. In fact, it would be wise to have that particular chimney torn out, though it will be a shame to destroy such good and lasting work. It is better than allowing unsuspecting new owners to risk misfortune."

Mr. Stone was patting his forehead with a white

handkerchief. It is quite difficult for people to alter their perception of what is possible and what is not in the space of a minute or two. So it is understandable if Mr. Stone was at that moment busily rationalizing in his own mind, convincing himself that he had witnessed nothing at all. For a moment I feared it would be rather difficult to convince him the old masonry must be removed despite the expense and bother.

But the hounds were not about to let him fool himself. They were apparently able to hear or sense my plan, though I'd foolishly operated under the assumption that they were aware only of the den itself. They were growling and howling something fierce. The whole house resonated with the sound of them. Mr. Stone grabbed me in his arms — an act of impropriety that clearly embarrassed him, for he let go at once. "It's quite all right to seek comfort from me if you need it, Mr. Stone," I said, easing his embarrassment. But before I could so much as pat his hand to calm him down, our trouble had arrived.

The hounds were across the hearth without question. The library was ablaze. Mr. Stone and I rushed to the doorway, but the two snarling hounds stood just beyond the threshold, looking most inhospitable.

They ran about with their thin little flame-tails tucked between their legs, leaping at the library shelves, the walls, setting everything in their wake afire. We watched those fiery hounds at their handiwork, both of us too dumbfounded to register our own terror, for we knew a firetruck could never arrive in time.

"It seems," I said to Mr. Stone, my tone one of extreme gravity, "that the hounds knew no fire would be built for them again, and this was their final opportunity to hold the library for themselves."

There was rather more weariness and sorrow in my voice than mere recorded words can tell you. Mr. Stone and I fled the burning house and called the fire department from the next estate. There was nothing left afterward, except three chimneys, and the third of those fell down a few days later. It was a good thing, after all, that I had wasted so much time reading rather than writing, for my work burned anyway.

It was hell reconstructing my notes so that I could finish, a year behind schedule, *Northwest Houses and Their Ghosts.* Emotionally I was too grievously stricken by the whole episode and simply could not include the events as a chapter or even a footnote. That may seem odd in light of what I did put in the book, much of it grimmer than the Elliott affair. I tell it to you not only because you are so dear a friend and correspondent, but because you share so many of my interests and views, and will surely understand my grief.

Think. If it were you and I that haunted that fireplace, wouldn't we have guarded that library as fanatically? With our antiquarian interests, I'm sure we would. But unlike the poor souls there, you and I have never had a suicidal notion. You would never think to hang yourself in jail, nor I to let myself die of pneumonia as a final protest. We might share their empathic identification between the terrifying nature of their spectral existence, and the content of those many terrifying volumes. But we could not consider an end to the books as a valid adjunct to the end of our personal horror.

I think I understand them. But I surely cannot forgive

them. For I cannot stop thinking about the books. Those wonderful old books!

Serene Omen of Death in the Pike Place Market

Penelope Pettiweather,
Seattle, Washington, USA

Cyril Nettelbaum,
Ouks, Westbourneshire,
England

Dear Cyril,

Your query to me, "What is the best known ghost in your city?" might have been answered twenty years ago, "None other than the Burnley School Ghost!" But nowadays the answer would have to be the ghostly Indian maiden at the Pike Place Sanitary Market, which many a tourist has heard about, and many a market worker has seen.

There are actually several spirits haunting the market. Rick Mann, for a long time considered "the keeper of the legends"—an eccentric who attended yard sales in a big black hearse—once told a Seattle *Times* columnist, "You really have to wonder if the whole place isn't haunted." He spoke of the "Fat Lady Ghost," a woman of about three hundred pounds who fell through the rotting floor of a café balcony, landing on a table of the main floor.

She was spotted a few times after her whimsically grisly demise, but no lasting tradition grew up around her.

A volunteer worker at Left Bank Books admitted to me that she no longer stayed in the shop after closing. She had once heard someone's slow, plodding, inexplicable footsteps moving back and forth in the upstairs room, though absolutely no one but herself was in the store. This may have been the same spirit seen a few years ago on an upper floor restaurant that was called Vitium Capitale. The ghost was observed by a Samoan cook who often opened or closed the restaurant alone. The figure stood before the beautifully multi-paned windows, gazing down at the market, or across the roof of the main market building to where the ferries were plainly visible. This spirit was an exceedingly tall black youth with dreadlocks, gaunt and morosely handsome. Another café has taken over the same location, up the staircase from Left Bank Books. No one who presently works there has seen the watchful spirit, so perhaps he has traveled onward or upward.

Two ghosts haunt the market's bead store. The famed Indian maiden drops by at three-month intervals. The other is a lonely, somewhat mischievous and surprisingly lively ghost who dwells in the store pretty much constantly. Lynn Roberts Hancock of the Craft Emporium and Bead Shop said, "The first time I knew he was there was when he came and did this," and she demonstrated by pulling on columnist Rick Anderson's sleeve.

One day, the spirit turned on her radio, for ghosts are frequently able to influence radios, record players, and taping devices — perhaps the intangibility of "sound" is something their own intangibility can most easily deal with. Hancock said, "I turned it off. He turned it back on. I unplugged it, *and it still played.* Then we put it in a box, *and it still played.* Then we put the box with the radio in it in a drawer. *It still played.*"

The ghost does display a great deal of personality. Once a very obnoxious customer had a small plastic fruit tossed at her. Hardly "mean spirited," but it got a point across. Hancock made some lame and hasty excuse that things were always falling off the ceiling, but the customer knew something was amiss. The ghost clearly felt a degree of proprietorship and didn't think his "employee" ought to be harassed by unreasonable people.

Occasionally the shop's ghost gets a little out of hand, knocking things awry, or pulling stunts like that with the radio. These events seem to occur whenever he has been overlooked for a long time. He acts up to gain attention and, having achieved it, settles down for a while. Hancock said, "I've adjusted. I am very comfortable with him these days."

The best-known and longest-persisting market ghost is definitely the Indian maiden. She was reported throughout the 1950s and many times since; she was probably seen in earlier decades as well, but I have not found a surviving record of it. By various witnesses' reports, she is sometimes transparent, sometimes more substantial but with a white light about her, and sometimes so tangible that she is taken for an ordinary living woman. When spoken to, she vanishes. Her hair is in braids that fall to her waist. She wears a floor-length dress and a shawl that was once brightly colored, but faded from long use.

Most reports claim she is in her twenties, but at least one person observed her to be elderly, with brown, crinkly skin. All agree her appearance is one of regal serenity, even beatitude. A relatively recent addition to her lore is that her name is Princess Angeline and she was the daughter of Chief Sealth, for whom our city is named.

This identification is only recently grafted onto this ghost, and I don't personally think it has much validity. Princess Angeline lived to a regal, beautiful old age and saw the town named for her father become a real city. In the early days of the now lamented Frederic and Nelson store, which was then on Second Avenue, Indians sat outside the store selling woven blankets and such. But Angeline was far too noble for such activity, which is why I reject the late-occurring legend that the Pike Place Indian Maiden is Angeline. Even in her lifetime, folk memory held that she had, in her youth, saved the city from an Indian attack. If this was untrue, she never corrected anyone, for it had become a tradition that the favor be returned to her, and many of the shop owners were in agreement that all her needs were to be met for her entire life. In consequence, she would go into Frederic's and similar stores and carry out as much as her arms could hold of fancy foods, knickknacks, and dresses. In consequence her house became jam-packed with wonderful and useless possessions. That's the real Princess Angeline, and I cannot see room in her history to account for her appearing as a young ghostly maiden.

By older tradition, which we may regard as better evidence, the ghost lived in the early 1900s, when the

Market was first established. In those days, she was one among the many independent merchants, and she sold handmade baskets, and several witnesses have reported that when she appeared, she was carrying her baskets. As the story goes, she vanished suddenly, and no one ever knew what became of her.

In 1983, Rick Anderson interviewed a man named Leon, who at the time purported to be the last living individual to have seen the Indian maiden. There were actually many sightings after Leon's 1963 experience, but not everyone at the market compares notes on these matters. Leon had a gift shop on the market's lower level. In those days, most sightings of the Indian woman were on or near the ramp leading to a branch of Goodwill Industries which in those days rented one of the largest spaces in the market. The ghost was also known to pass straight through walls, apparently adhering to corridors that alterations of the market's configuration had closed off or eradicated.

Leon was standing in the hallway with three other shopkeepers when the ghost passed right by them on her way to the Goodwill ramp. She looked like a normal person to Leon, but the others were very startled by her. One of his fellow merchants said, "That's her. That's the ghost."

"Pshaw," said Leon, and separated from his friends immediately in an effort to catch the woman and prove her to be tangible. He had not followed very far when she vanished in the blink of an eye. Leon still couldn't believe it, and went so far as to ask a woman to check the ladies' bathroom to see if the Indian maiden was somewhere about. "But she just wasn't there," Leon afterward admitted. "I'd seen her walk by my shop before. Although she seemed somewhat odd, moving slowly as if her feet barely touched the floor, and never turned her head, I hadn't thought much about her. She seemed perfectly human. She was rather large, with grayish black hair. But when I really thought about it, she *had* always been strange. Her long dress changed colors in a mysterious way, first lavender, then pink."

There had long been a belief that all who saw the serene Indian maiden were destined for a violent death, though not necessarily right away. Informant Rick Mann reported that it was extremely unlucky to see her. Of the three people who were with Leon on the day he tried to catch up with the ghost, he said, "Bill had a heart attack. Marie committed suicide. And Ruth was murdered." As for Leon, Rick Anderson tried a few years later to do a follow-up interview — and discovered Leon was missing. His fate remains unknown.

Reporter Paul Andrews investigated the market ghosts in October of 1983 for *Parade Magazine*, and found that most people believed the Indian woman made her rounds frequently, but only after the lights were out and the market closed for the night, or she would be seen even more often. For all the bustle, noise, and color of the market's working hours, it does close early, and becomes a series of gloomy, windswept semi-open-air hallways, sectioned by chain gratings on the upper level, by fire doors on the lower. There is limited access even to merchants, and few would ever have the chance to see the maiden and to fall under her sorrowful curse.

No one actually believes she is malignant, because she

appears so beatific. Supposedly, those doomed to deaths as tragic as her own are more susceptible to seeing her, but she in no way causes their fates. Many people have observed her and are alive to tell of it—but since there is no time limit on the purported curse, they could live to be ninety, die of pneumonia or a car accident, and blame the death on the maiden.

I for one never believed she was malignant, or I would not have made the effort I made to communicate with this spirit. I had every expectation of coming face to face with her, and no fear of dropping dead as a result. I worked one summer at Shakespeare and Company Books on one of the lower levels of the market, and often had occasion to stay late, eagerly awaiting her presence.

I talked to many fellow marketers about the maiden. Those who bore witness to her existence were not really scared they were doomed for having seen the beautiful spirit, but they were aware of the past deaths, and so often had little twinges of worry.

After the Goodwill closed its market branch, and that space was renovated, the Indian maiden began to haunt another inside level. She took an especial liking to Lynn Hancock's bead store, which is down a dead-end corridor, with windows overlooking Puget Sound. Lynn said, "She was standing back there looking at seed-beads. I walked back and said, 'May I help you?' and she was gone. It was like she was never there."

After the Indian disappeared, Hancock was shaken enough to close her store. She stood outside near the restroom and wondered if she had been hallucinating. "I thought, 'I've been working too hard.'" But it happened again, and other workers in the shop spotted the ghost as well. Because of the fear that surrounded her appearance—the purported violent deaths that followed sightings—Hancock was taking no chances. An Indian shaman was brought in to put a Circle of Protection around the bead store. "He had an eagle-feather fan and sage and sweet grass. Both my kids were here, and we went through the ceremony."

Protective sage hangs in the shop to this day. If that spectral Indian maiden ever was really the source of dangerous curses, the efforts of the knowledgeable medicine man have surely restrained the ill effects of seeing her. The ghost continued to appear in three-month cycles, and Lynn personally observed her a half-dozen times in the following years. Never again were untoward deaths credited to the maiden's appearance, and what could be more sweetly touching than a ghost's continued interest in Indian seed beads?

One night I had stayed late in the bookshop to organize shelves. It had been a hot summery day, and the south wing of the lower level held the muggy heat all evening. I was on a high ladder alphabetizing sundry titles; up near the ceiling, the heat was even more unbearable. Yet without preamble, I felt a sudden chill, and immediately climbed down from the ladder to see if the fire door exit had been opened by someone, though it is supposed to be locked after hours.

I found it was indeed still locked. Where had the cool draft come from?

I looked south along the darkened corridor, and saw a faint glow moving away. I hurried after it. The light was a faint blue shifting to lavender. "Hello!" I called, but the shimmering Indian woman did not look back. I called again, "Wait!" and my voice echoed in the empty corridor. She moved steadily but slowly, and I was closing on her. She went up the staircase to the next level of the market. I hurried up the stairs and saw that she was heading up the ramp toward the Sound View Café, holding a basket in her arms.

I focused all my attention upon her, knowing she was apt at any time to vanish. I was trying to "hold her fast," as one tries to hold onto a dream upon waking. By this method I was able to keep her in sight. She went right by the Sound View and started down another stairway. The steps were wide enough that I could walk right beside her. She was oblivious to my presence.

We came to the back entry of the day care center, which is in part of the old Goodwill space. She walked straight through a closed doorway. It was locked after hours, so I could no longer follow, and felt a terrible sense of loss that this was so.

I peered through a small glass window and saw her striding down the slanted floor. I sent my thoughts after her, trying my hardest to establish some communication—and briefly, I succeeded. She stopped, turned slowly, and gazed at me through the glass.

In her gaze, I felt engulfed by overwhelming serenity. I experienced a sense of reassurance such as I can never describe. She then showed me the contents of her basket, which was a pure light. In that moment she had ceased to be an Indian maiden, for she had herself become part of the pure light. Out of that brightness there issued—how can I say it? I was so profoundly affected, I thought surely I was viewing a manifestation of Divine Love, and really wondered if I weren't in the presence of a Goddess.

Then the light was gone. Nothing of the ghost remained, and I was panting with a kind of desire to possess that light.

As you well know, Cyril, I am no novice when it comes to hauntings. But this one really was different. I hardly dare to try to make sense of it. Had I been in China, I would have sworn I'd been visited by Kuan Yin, Goddess of Compassion. As it is, she will always be an enigma to me. All I know is that even now, when I think of her basket full of light, all the sad feelings of life are shunted aside, and all fear of death eases away. I welcome your thoughts about her.

Thine affectionately,
Penelope

The Spirit Shaman of Glen Acres Golf Course

Penelope Pettiweather,
Kelowna, British Columbia,
Canada

Jane Bradshaw,
Oundle, Northants,
England

Dear Jane,

You asked, in my haunted adventures, if I hadn't encountered a Native American ghost. It's not easy to answer directly. By and large that's quite an old fashioned sort of ghost, and for decades beginning in earliest settlements in the Pacific Northwest, the most common kind of ghost sightings were Indian ghosts.

But those sorts of ghosts seem to have become passé, which for most would be a clue that ghosts aren't real, or every generation wouldn't have a different sort. But you and I know ghosts are very real, and my own sense of their having "fashions" of one kind and then another, is that they transmute with time. We only partially understand who or what they are, and whatever holds them at their root, it is perceived by each of us according to the dictates of a given tradition, and our minds "fill them in" in ways we find at least marginally comprehensible.

Compared to your countryside, inhabited by your own race since time immemorial, you might well encounter ghosts of your own ancestors. But for the white settlers in the Northwest, who didn't arrive in great numbers until the 1800s, in order to have ghosts of a greater past requires that they be Native Americans. But by now, even with a scant two centuries of history, whites can perceive the world of the unreal more and more as a mirror of ourselves, and only Indians perceive ghosts as Indians.

And another point, to do with the fashion of a politic, once it was commonplace to tell stories of Indian ghosts around campfires because Indians seemed exotic and fantastical, even alive, let alone as spirits. Nowadays, the first peoples are our friends, neighbors, or at the very least our table dealers at casinos on Reservations. They're no more exotic than anyone. Plus some few take exceptions to being the brunt of exotic tales! So there are pressures to tell a mere campfire ghost story without offense.

It remains, the fuller history of Puget Sound is Indian history, not white. That a smaller percentage of local ghost sightings are of Indians, that's something we may lament, for it may well be that this is due to the sweeping away of Native American history, inadequately taught in our schools. And the few Native Americans who preserve native ways and myths and religion don't necessarily want to share it outside their community, much as whites do love to have Native spirituality monetized for our own benefit. And so Native spirits fade along with knowledge of the people.

Yet some Indian ghosts do linger in the folk memory, such as the Omen Maiden who still walks the Pike Place Market. The Market is unique in that it is a continuous culture unto itself from the early 1900s to the present, each generation of merchants overlapping sufficiently to carry traditions along the decades. Elsewhere, many traditional tales are being lost because people live in places so transiently, and because the art of storytelling has been displaced by televisions and cinema and simple-minded memes on the World Wide Web.

Fifty years ago or so, Indian ghosts were still the most usual kind. In 1929, developers turned a patch of forest at 10th South and South 110th into a golf course. Shortly afterward, the spirit of an Indian shaman began to manifest there, reaching his peak of notice from the 1950s through the '70s. Many people saw him, and the police were often called in to try and run him off the course. From that spirit's point of view, rituals were required to run off the invasive pale beings he perceived as mightily unpleasant interlopers, i.e., duffers.

The Glendale Golf and Country Club is still there, though it is now called the Glen Acres Country Club. It is a handsome combination of lawn and semi-woodland, with many of the old trees still standing. The clubhouse is a beautiful chateau. It unequivocally evokes the mood of a haunted place.

Interest in the Club's ghost survives, and they have printed up a one-page handout that both answers re-curring questions, and keeps the tradition alive. For those of us who love folklore and ghostly tales, and hate to see them pass away into rational and technological modernity, we can be grateful that the Glen Acres ghost is still treated as worthy of commentary at the old chateau. Even so, the last authentic sighting—if we discount some rather inebriated exceptions on the part of the tipsier club members—seems to have been in the 1970s, when decades of continuous sightings were recalled, and hundreds of people admitted to having seen the apparition.

Why did this Indian, a relic of the past, appear "suddenly" with the opening of a golf course? Was he "disturbed" from long rest by development of the land? Had he always been there, performing his ghostly rituals hidden amidst the trees, his doings rendered visible only after a part of the forest was carted away to make room for expansive lawns?

As a symbol of the landscape's past, he was marvelous. He was a sorrowfully romantic reminder that the encroachment of civilization had become so utter and annihilating that nothing truly wild persists. Duffers drove their golf carts on a vast lawn that once was a wilderness—probably sacred land such as Indians thought would be eternal, and might've been in their care. Who better than the Native American to invoke pity for the loss of such beauty in the Northwest?

I do sometimes feel I've lived too long, for I find myself saying more and more, "I remember when." I remember when you couldn't walk two hundred paces in any direction without standing amidst trees and wild birds; when you couldn't walk four hundred paces without encountering a clear freshwater brook. Every dairy, bean-field and homestead of South King County was formerly surrounded by woods. Even the drive along Highway 99 between Seattle and Tacoma provided an excursion through forests. Now, most of the dairies and bean-fields have passed away from this once scenic drive, let alone the forests, and in their place we have endless miles of new and used car lots, mobile home parks, tract housing, strip malls and shopping centers, and, yes, the occasional golf course.

Where, in all this, could anything spiritual find its moment of peace? For that matter, where amidst so much concrete can anything *human* find peace? Well, a golf course just might be the best bet after all, especially on a rainy winter near dusk, with only the staunchest of duffers around, when the fine greenery and quietude makes an ancient shaman feel almost as though his whole world lives anew.

Such at least was the preferred haunting grounds of the Green Acres spirit-shaman. He usually appeared a few feet in the air, where the ground had been before developers leveled it. He danced wildly and, but for a tubular headdress, he wore absolutely no clothes, but was painted with spots and wavy lines of white and black and grey. He twisted and gyrated, and, although it was clear from his face that he was chanting quite as wildly as he was dancing, there issued from him no sound at all.

Those duffers who refused to believe in ghosts thought him an exhibitionist of some sort, and called the police. It was a private club, after all, and lunatics with unpaid dues were not welcome. No "flasher" wearing nothing but body paint was ever corralled. The police would converge, at various intervals, hoping to prove via arrest that the spirit-shaman was a clever but ordinary man. But the shaman invariably vanished just as they were upon him.

It came to be believed that the Glen Acres golf course had once been a sacred Indian burial ground, though no one could possibly know that. In this sad and swiftly changing world, it is certainly easy to imagine the wild dance and the silent chanting of a spirit-shaman are more rather than less required, if only for the sake of dreamy imagination. His efforts are necessary, in order to purify daily sacrileged holy soil. We may only wish for a spiritual leader in our own afterlife to care for us so greatly.

Love,
Penelope

The Forest in the Lake

Penelope Pettiweather,
Seattle, Washington, USA

Cyril Nettelbaum,
Ouks, Westbourneshire,
England

Dear Cyril,

Why, of course, when you make your journey from your beloved shires of England to the equally misty Pacific Northwest of America, I will certainly house you. What sort of friend would your old Penelope be, otherwise? There's no sense spending extravagant fees at a bed-and-breakfast when you've a friend in the vicinity. As for your overly cautious fretting of what my neighbors might say about me if an old English bachelor spent a week or so with an old American bachelorette — well, Cyril, to tell the truth, it rather appeals to me that any neighbor of mine could actually suppose, after all these years, I've finally gotten up the nerve to become an old sinner.

The "true" legends you recounted to me in your last letter, regarding British lake monsters, were delightful, and they have gone straight into my "collection" of strange-but-true accounts of haunted or strangely inhabited waterways the world over. You're quite right. The Northwest has its share of traditional beasties of a similar type, dwelling along the ocean's coast, the Straits of Juan de Fuca, the sound, and in every lake hereabouts. In Lake Steilacoom near Tacoma, the evil Whe-atchee, a female monster, dwells under the water, so that the Nisqually Indians refused to fish or swim there. Fish Lake near Mount Adams had a dragon in it that hid behind a door in the bed of the lake. The Klickitat Indians would not eat fish from that lake and shunned it generally. Rain spirits dwelt in all the lakes between Mount Adams and Mount Rainier, these being benevolent and respected; but the rain spirits hated noise and if their quietude was disrupted, the next rain would be an awful storm.

There was a serpent monster big enough to swallow canoes in Lake Quinault on the Olympic Peninsula, battled by the heroic figure Kwatee the Changer. Spirit Lake of Mount Saint Helens was the abode of numerous evil spirits, and Indians rarely hunted near it, claiming they heard demonic noises in the lake — which obviously was the rumbling of that very active volcano. The Spirit Lake monsters were called Seatco and were known to drag fishermen to the bottom. A ghost elk was credited with luring hunters to Spirit Lake so the Seatco could get them, for the Indian method of hunting was to drive elk into the water. One creature dwelling there was an enormous fish with a bear's head and it ate people. There are literally hundreds of stories like these!

But some of the strange tales of the Great Northwest's aquatic oddities are not legends at all, but bold facts of science that *ought* to be legends even when they aren't.

For instance, the biggest octopi in the world are not found in the depths of the Indian Ocean or in some other far tropical waters. They're right here in Puget Sound. Scuba divers say the giant octopus is a whimsical fellow who likes to play, shy at first, but very trusting and curious if given the chance. Some of these clever beasties have learned that divers thrash about in a most wonderful and entertaining manner if the octopus entwines itself in the diving gear and commences to disconnect the hoses. When an octopus "laughs," the colors shift along its body, just like a blushing person.

The intelligence of these creatures is suggested by a half-grown and very friendly octopus who lived at the old Seattle Aquarium. This was back in the days of the famed Namu and other killer whales. In those days the aquarium was certainly not the state-of-the-art affair it is today. It had a quaint side-show atmosphere. Visitors were encouraged to feed the seals bits of fish purchased for the purpose, and a series of short-lived whales in undersized pools were each in turn eager to stick their fins out of the water to "shake hands." Strictly as an aside, I had gotten a crush on a whale called Kandu, and if no one was watching, I was able to coax her to me. I actually kissed her snout on several occasions. The tragedy and the beauty of their captive personalities was really very touching. They did so poorly in small pools, it was certainly a good idea to stop capturing them.

Back then the aquarium was located entirely at the end of a pier otherwise taken up by Pirate's Plunder, the import concern. For several weeks the workers were puzzled as to what had been happening to their blue crabs. Each time they replenished the supply, the crabs would be picked off mysteriously a few each night, with only their empty shells left behind. Then one night a worker "caught" a certain octopus, who lived about four tanks away from the crabs, going about one of his midnight sorties. This fellow could squeeze his body out of a surprisingly small hole—far too small, by appearances, for any octopus to get through—and then he crawled across the top of the tanks until it got to the blue crabs' home. He would then squeeze through another small hole, eat a few crabs, and return by the same route, leaving no clue regarding his nightly endeavors. The thing is, when the octopus was finally caught in the act, he made a valiant effort to get out of the blue crab tank and back to his own home as quickly as possible, like a dog caught chewing his master's slippers and striving against all hope to deny his part in it.

Back in the 1970s, the Point Defiance Aquarium in Tacoma used to keep a couple of giant octopi out where they could be petted. Because the octopus is so sensitive in captivity, the aquarium no longer does this. Even back then, there was a sign on the pool of each that read, "Do Not Touch the Octopus." But it was impossible not to do so. Those big things were *tame.* They *wanted* you to touch them. How could a visitor resist? And, once again, if you can believe it, these creatures seemed genuinely to love practical jokes.

One octopus would come to the far side of the top of its pool and hang from the rim. It would reach one of its great huge tentacles across the surface toward the clutch of observers, using the very tip of its tentacle like a little finger calling "come hither." Children and adults alike easily recognized what that motion meant, and were tempted to touch the tentacle, but were usually reluctant and tentative about it, for they could never be sure the big monster didn't actually want to eat them.

In fact, the octopus had no intention of hurting anybody. Despite the parrot-like beak in the center of that tangle of arms, it's rare for them to bite even when frightened. That Point Defiance octopus genuinely liked to be petted, and his "come hither" was a seriously intended ploy to gain physical contact with humanity. I suppose it sounds quite fantastic if you've never acquired any knowledge of octopi in the sea or in captivity; but take Penelope's solemn oath, these beasts are as wise and affectionate, in their own way, as anyone's dog or cat. And if you and I were a sea-dwelling merman and mermaid, surely we'd have octopi as our companions.

As weirdly smart as the octopus is, the park's seductive fellow understood full well that people who didn't know its personality were *scared* to touch it even if they were tempted.

Picture if you will the child or adult who slowly, slowly, ever so slowly reaches closer and closer to that "come hither" tentacle. The tentacle, too, moved slowly, slowly — until the human hand touches the water, then zap!, the octopus reaches out rapidly and grabs the hand! That hand comes out of that pool as fast as lightning, accompanied by a loud yelp of surprise. And the octopus begins to "laugh" its blushing laugh.

I would visit that very octopus at least once a month, and I saw it pull this stunt dozens of times. It clearly knew what it was up to. But whenever somebody failed to jerk away, and wasn't afraid, the octopus was eager to befriend the visitor. It would grab hold of the entire hand, and pull itself to the side of the pool nearest the newfound friend. Its coloration would lighten, and it would grow perfectly calm to be petted.

These octopi recognized their keepers, and liked some of them better than others. They knew who had the food and who didn't; who would play with them and who wouldn't. They also "played" with objects, just as would a cat. Most scientists think they're very short lived in the wild, which is truly sad, because they obviously love life. Out in the sound, they build houses of stones, and prefer to make them from the prettiest rocks. They collect useless objects, especially shiny bits of metal and smoothed glass, to keep in their houses. To tell the truth, I rather relate to their view of the world, living as I do amidst my own accumulation of quaint clutter.

These boneless beasts learn a great deal, and store up a lot of knowledge, for they have the ability to "remember" things they're only reminded of occasionally and have no intrinsic need to know. This may all sound fantastic, but every word is true; get any modern octopus book out of your library, and you'll find many things even more remarkable about the animal.

All this tentacled wit and wisdom has to be crowded into a life span of only about seven years. That saddens me quite a bit, for our own lives of seventy or eighty years seem so very short, and here is an animal that delights in its world who lives very briefly indeed. However, some recent investigators at the University of Washington are of the opinion that the Puget Sound giant octopus may actually live quite a bit longer than previously supposed; it is only those that live in captivity who succumb quickly.

Yet another "strange but true" bit of Northwest natural history regards the underwater forest in Lake Washington. The lake is not only the largest in Western Washington, it happens to be one of the deepest lakes in the United States. It is two hundred feet down in places, with another hundred feet of silt—three hundred feet to solid ground, and exceedingly cold both because of the depth and the water feeding in from the mountain glaciers. Nevertheless, the area of Lake Washington was once a deep valley with no water in it at all, except for some little streams, I suppose.

The shifts that land can make are extremely slow. By increments over thousands or even millions of years, the valley became sealed on all sides, and then filled with water. It happened so slowly that the valley forests adjusted to their new environment! Those "antediluvian" fir forests are still down there, and in a few places from a boat, you can see the tops of the trees reaching for the light, never quite breaking the surface of the water.

One of my uncles—Wilson, not the eccentric Elvin—was a scuba diver in the navy many years ago. After he left the navy, he taught scuba diving lessons, oh, way back in the '60s and '70s. He was the first person to tell me how some of the octopi in Puget Sound that had gotten to "understand" divers and liked to get on top of them and unplug their equipment, just for fun.

Scuba divers don't usually like the lakes, because they're much dirtier than the sea, and it's harder to keep one's equipment cleared of floating plants. But Wilson had heard about the submerged forest and wanted to see it for himself. Soon he was out there in Lake Washington, and though it's a whole lot cleaner than it was a great many years ago when sewage was dumped right into it, you just never get the kind of clarity you do in Puget Sound.

Therefore Wilson was right amidst the forest before he realized it, for the trees had not been visible until he was quite close to them. He was disappointed that the trees were extremely raggedy and not very attractive. Some hardly looked like they were still alive. He swam around several of them. They were gigantic, and their bark was sturdy; they were in no way decayed or rotten. Clearly they *were* still alive, even if their needles were awfully skimpy. Most of the few needles were to be found near the tops of the long trunks.

Then he saw something odd in the shadowy underwater fir forest. There appeared to be a scrap of trawler's net strung between two trees. The net stretched from the silt nearly to the top of the trees to which it was snagged. It almost looked like a spider's web, with eight enormous threads converging on a center. Trawling was illegal in the lake, and Wilson's first thought was that whoever lost this net must have dumped it overboard on purpose when spotted by a patrol boat.

As he approached the strange net, he saw that the great knot in the center was alive. His heart began to palpitate with wonder, for he had been diving long enough to know there were no fleshy creatures like that anywhere in the Northwest, and certainly nothing that made fat, stringy webs! But undeniably that one gigantic eyeball was peering at him through the water's haze. Wilson drifted there, gazing back at that enormous eye, until slowly it dawned on him where he had seen just such a sight.

It was the eye of an octopus! But the eight legs, which he had mistaken for some kind of netting, were far too skinny to be those of an ordinary octopus. And although the biggest octopi in the world were in Puget Sound, they did not live in fresh water; and they weren't even half as big as the monster in front of him now.

But if trees could adjust to living under water, then assuredly a special strain of octopus might adapt to fresh water, if it had thousands of years to evolve and make the adjustment. It was feasible that a colony of Puget Sound octopi were cut off from the sound ages ago, and, as their salt lake became purified over time by the influx of freshwater, this strain adapted. They changed over the generations until they were even larger than their giant cousins in the sound. Their bodies became fatter, their tentacles longer and thinner, like ropes. And if they dwelt in the siltier places of Lake Washington, no one would ever see or catch them in the hundred feet of muck wherein they raised their families.

Wilson knew that it was the nature of the octopus to be shy, unless his trust was won, and then the creature was friendly and mischievous. They were never dangerous. But this one was so enormous, perhaps it wouldn't behave like a normal octopus. Perhaps he, Wilson, looked like a tasty little morsel! He was torn between his fear and his curiosity. He wanted to swim away as fast as he could, but he also wanted to get nearer to the thing to find out if it was truly real.

Kicking his flippers lightly, Wilson glided toward the beastly apparition. The great eye rotated to watch him. Then one of those long, ropy tentacles came loose from the limb to which it had been clinging, and reached for of the scuba diver—slowly, slowly, closer and closer. It was not a threatening motion, but indicated curiosity. The coloration slowly changed in waves or bands, like a great dark rainbow of grays and browns and faint pinks rippling through its body.

Just before the tip of the tentacle touched him, Wilson panicked. He thrashed the water to get away from the monster, and pulled his diving knife from its strap at his heel. The enormous, spidery octopus responded in kind. All the tentacles came loose from the trees, and seemed to partially retract into the bulbous body. Then with a jet of ink, the creature shot away like a dart.

Too late, Wilson regretted himself. He followed the trail of ink through the water until it faded away, the track leading into the deeper waters where a diver couldn't reach, and toward an area of deep silt.

Wilson explored the area as deep as he dared to go, until his tank was too nearly out of air for him to continue. At one point, he spied a curious arrangement of stones poking up from the silt in one place, causing Wilson to imagine a stone-built "city" under the mud. But he saw no evidence of the creature.

In weeks and months to come, and for several years to follow, he returned again and again to the underwater forest, always taking special camera equipment with him. But never again did a friendly tentacle reach forth in curiosity to welcome the diver.

Thine obediently,
Penelope

The Oval Dragon

Penelope Pettiweather,
Seattle, Washington, USA

Jane Bradshaw,
Oundle, Northants,
England

Dear Jane,

I'm glad you liked that "fish story" (or should I say "octopus story") which Cyril put in the last number of his little magazine. Your passing nit about "octopuses" or "octopedes" being the proper plurals, rather than "octopi," is well taken. I can see that a Greek word with a Latin plural would sound odd to a language expert. But to mere Americans, "octopi" has become so common that it sounds right to us, even if it is absurd.

I've been collecting these serpenty tales for some time now (and you thought I only liked ghosts!). So I was delighted to get the added tale of "the squishy thing from the loch" of your experience. You ask if I have personally seen any sea serpents, and I regret to say I have not—not yet, at least. But do remind me I should write you sometime about a gigantic, barnacle-encrusted sea maiden I saw near the Swinomish Reservation.

I've been trying for some while to meet one of these

beasties and have based several camping trips on legends I've heard about. A lake near the Cascade foothills by Mount Adams was previously ruled by a gigantic swan queen named Hawelakok. She used to let people use the water from her lake, but stirred it up to drown whoever tried to take fish from it. There are Indian kelpies as well—like the American Lake spotted ghost horse which grabs swimmers and drowns them.

You ask if anyone here ever "fakes" sea serpents, as is often done in sundry Scottish lochs to draw tourism. To my knowledge, this has never been done locally. Despite a great many lake-monster legends throughout the Northwest, no one has cashed in on them for tourist value. Since *authentic* lore has been for the most part ignored, I suppose there's just no "market" for fakery. I can't recall any incidents such as the event you recount, of that group of duffers who actually built an elaborate hoax serpent to troll about in the lake mists. Fishermen certainly do tell whopping tales about things they've nearly captured, but no one has yet reported to me any elaborate hoaxes attendant to their tales. Perhaps most of us Americans lack the British wit to invent, and imagination to believe. On the other hand, we *do* have, on the Columbia River, a Druid style "folly" in the form of a perfect replica of Stonehenge put up by a wealthy eccentric, Sam Hill. He unfortunately didn't have the monument built facing the right direction, so it's useless for equinoctial observances.

In America, I think it is much more common to fake flying saucers than ghosts or lake monsters. I recall in the '70s there was a flying saucer convention here in

Seattle, and one evening a couple of good ol' boys let loose some weather balloons with traffic flares dangling off them. About fifty UFO conventioneers had such "believing" mindsets that they were thoroughly convinced they'd shared a mass sighting, until the traffic flare melted part of one of the balloons and it fell amidst them.

I must say, though, that there are some examples of fishermen's lore that do make one pause to wonder. The *usual* point of a good fish story is to credit oneself for nearly bagging the biggest one that ever got away. But even the most inveterate of liars, such as all fishermen are, set limitations on what they feel the listener is gullible enough to believe. The purpose of the lie is altogether lost if the teller seeks anonymity. Even so, the teller of one curious tale, first recorded in the Tacoma *Daily Ledger* way back on July 3, 1893, wished his name not to be revealed, for it was a whale of a tale he might justifiably expect never to be believed.

The fisherman who first told the tale to the *Ledger's* reporter a century ago was an easterner, which, in those days, was often thought sufficient to explain a lunatic character. He and three other men set out from Tacoma on a three-day fishing tour of the sound. "Our party was supplied with the necessaries of life as well as an abundance of its luxuries," the easterner reported, the "luxuries" including whiskey and rye. He said, "But it must not be inferred from this fact that the luxuries played any part in creating the sights seen on that memorable outing. We left Tacoma on July first, Saturday, about four-thirty in the afternoon and, as the wind was from the southeast, we shaped our course for Point Defiance."

They fished at Point Defiance for a while, then tried their hand at a Henderson Island trout stream that poured into Black Fish Bay, the name "black fish" alluding to the orca whales that visit these waters even today. The geological features of the sea floor are unusual at this location, and the waters in this area are extraordinarily deep.

The men camped the night on the island, having imbibed sufficiently that their wits were undoubtedly a bit dulled. Thus their ensuing adventure had an edge of drunken unreality about it, and we can only speculate as to what percentage of their experience was misunderstood by themselves in their varied states of inebriation.

Along about midnight, a frightful noise awoke the four men, a crackling sound accompanied by a stinging sensation, like thousands of little needles stabbing them through their blankets and clothes. This very sensation has in recent times been caused by electrical "leaks" into the ground from high voltage wires, and has caused pets and farm animals to leap straight up from the ground, and cows to stop giving milk or even to be killed. But in 1893, the phenomenon could hardly have been blamed on high voltage wires, there being none on Henderson Island. Had things stopped at this point, we might easily have supposed the little camp had just survived being struck by lightning. Things did not stop at that, but progressed weirdly.

The easterner said, "The air was filled with a strong

current of electricity that caused every nerve in the body to sting with pain. A light as bright as that created by a concentration of many arc lights kept constantly flashing. I turned my head in that direction, and if it is possible for fright to turn a man's hair white, then mine ought to be white now."

Fortunately for him, the easterner still had black hair. Had the phenomenon been lightning-related, he might well have been rendered bald, for those struck by lightning are known sometimes to lose every hair on their head, never to re-grow it.

"There before my eyes," the fisherman continued, "was a most horrible looking monster. The monster slowly drew in toward shore and, as it approached, its head poured out a stream of water that looked like blue flame."

The amazing story, it might appear, regarded some heretofore unknown species of electric fish, for we may recall that electric eels put out enough current to shock a man to death. The holiday fisherman reported that it was one hundred feet long, and thirty feet in circumference. "Its shape was somewhat out of the ordinary insofar as the body was neither round nor flat, but oval. It had coarse hair on the upper body. At about every eight feet from its head to its tail, a substance that had the appearance of a copper band encircled it. Blue flames came from two horn-like structures near the center of the head. The tail was shaped like a propeller."

Now from the "hair" we could suppose either sea algae, which is known to adhere to certain sea animals, or else the oval monster was a mammal. It is perfectly feasible that one hundred years ago, remnants of the once-plentiful giant sea cow, hunted to extinction by whalers, had found its way to Black Fish Bay. As for the horn, the narwhale sports a single horn, and many species of fish and reptile sport one or more horns. The copper bands would seem to be only coloration, a striped animal being common enough, unless we are speaking of something literally metallic that aided in the manufacture or conduction of electricity.

"Sir, I tell you, in the electrically charged atmosphere birds and insects died. Two of my fellow fishermen became paralyzed when licked by the blue flame. They lay on the beach until eventually recovered. At last, the monster submerged into the dark waters and a tell-tale light betrayed its course. I hardly need tell you we were not long getting underway for Tacoma, and I can assure you I may no more desire to fish in waters of this bay. There are too many peculiar inhabitants in them."

When we resort to science, the first response to this story is to say it is an impossibility. Certainly no such animal is known, and if it did once exist, it must now be extinct. Luminous fish, some of monstrous size, are known to students of ocean life, and occasionally there are reports of strange sea monsters washed ashore here and there. The report of a "furred" quality to the beast reminds us that from Alaska to the Northwest there are many reports of gigantic long-necked seals which were the mammalian equivalents of the plesiosaurs. No specialist in the sea will deny that it is filled with species uncataloged and occasionally strange beasts have washed ashore on various coasts, decayed by the time scientists investigate, so that the mysteries remain irresolvable.

In the last century and this, there have been many sightings of such sea creatures in Puget Sound and the Strait of Juan de Fuca. None repeated the feature of the Oval Dragon of Point Defiance; none spouted electrified water. If the four men were hoaxed, they were hoaxed well. If they were fully inebriated by their admitted "luxuries," then pray tell, how did they hallucinate the same experience together?

As you can see, Jane, I've pondered this old tale from every possible angle in an attempt to surmise whether or not there is any chance it actually happened as reported. Your account of a loch serpent hoax caused me to think of this old report, and I do wonder if the four fishermen weren't the victims of some dangerous mistake, if not exactly a hoax.

Perhaps the most believable explanation was that the Oval Dragon was actually a mechanical device, such as fascinated Victorians generally. It wouldn't take a mad scientist, but only an eccentric inventor, to build in secret an electrically-driven ship shaped generally like a fat serpent. Several elements of the eyewitness description suggests a human contrivance of this sort. The "propeller" shaped tail may indeed have been a propeller. The two spewing horns may have been exhaust pipes. The copper bands may have been part of a primitive electrical generator. Its mouth, which spewed blue water, may have been only the result of a hand-operated water pump which had the perfectly utilitarian purpose of keeping the vessel afloat. The very oval fatness of the serpent implies a hull of some sort.

Such a ship might well, like the ironclad monitors

built as early as the Civil War, ride so low in the water as to nearly resemble a submarine. And its passenger-inventor would ride inside, unseen by observers and probably unable to see the camping fishermen in the darkness outside the vessel. The act of pumping water out the mouth of the figurehead would have caused the low-riding vessel to lurch upward, and it would certainly be a shocking thing to fishermen who were sleepy and possibly a bit tipsy viewing it in the starlight.

It's only my theory, but I like to envision within the Oval Serpent the passenger-inventor sitting at the controls, like a character out of a Jules Verne novel, pumping water from his electric ironclad. It was a test ride rather than a hoax, but had the same effect. By accident the inventor nearly electrocuted the startled campers.

It's an amusing theory, but it almost demands a sad conclusion. As his invention was never revealed to the world at large, it may well be that he succeeded in electrocuting himself by means of the same electrical discharge experienced by the fishermen even on dry land. He fried himself crisp as a chip inside his ship, which sank in the unnaturally deep waters never again to be seen—save only by the orcas and the octopi (or octopuses).

Love,
Penelope

The Woman Who Turned to Soap

"An old legend has it that Lake Crescent never gives up its dead. The Klallams would never cross it by canoe. They said there were evil spirits that reached upward with icy claws to drag down anyone who tried to fish there. Until 1957, the lake was commonly thought to be bottomless; many grew up in Port Angeles believing that was a fact. It was finally sounded at six hundred twenty-four feet at its deepest point; and that's plenty deep enough."

The waitress seemed to have taken her break specifically to fill me in on the local lore. She had overheard me introducing myself to the bartender as "Penelope Pettiweather, intrepid Northwest folklorist and ghost detective." He'd laughed, glad enough to meet an eccentric old gal with an interest in strange things, but he couldn't add much to my store of notes. I hadn't seen the young woman as the bartender and I spoke, but when I sat down at a table with a Roy Rogers and a grilled cheese sandwich to peruse my field notes, the waitress sat across from me and said, "You're the woman who writes books of spooky stories for kids?"

"Well, not necessarily for children, but I must confess I do write about odd things now and then. Call me

Penny."

"Hi, Penny, glad to meet you," she said, offering me a hand across the table. She didn't introduce herself. "Are those notes about the soap woman?"

"Some are. Do you know anything about her?"

"Sure." She lit up a cigarette. I wished she hadn't, but you can't criticize someone who's about to volunteer sought-for information. She said, "I kind of relate to her in a weird way, you know what I mean? I think she wants her story remembered. She doesn't want to be forgotten. I've sort of taken it as my duty to keep her memory alive. I look like her a bit, don't you think?"

"I haven't seen a photo of her yet. I planned to spend the night here at the lodge and check local newspaper morgues and libraries tomorrow. Then I suppose I'll see some photos."

"Take my word for it; she and I could be sisters," she said, and leaned back in her seat. She blew smoke rings toward the ceiling, which rather impressed me despite my disapproval of smoking. My friendly waitress continued: "Hallie Illingsworth had auburn hair and piercing dark eyes. She was a big strong woman—not unattractive, mind you; but it couldn't have been easy killing her, I'll tell you that; she would have put up a devil of a fight. If not for a lucky blow, it might have been a husband rather than a wife that went into the bottom of that lake. So, what do your notes say there?" She was trying to read my scrawls upside down.

I lifted my notes. I began to read a fragment: "1940, afternoon of July 6—Lake Crescent for the first time returns one of its dead."

"You've got that right," she interrupted. "The first and

only time. The day she resurfaced, the lake was smooth as a mirror and the deepest blue imaginable, fading toward shore to a polished turquoise. There was this guy named Louis Rolfe in a fishing skiff with his brother. Louis spotted an oblong object and pointed it out. His brother asked, 'What the hell is it?' It floated near the rocky wall that leads to Sledgehammer Point. It looked like a human body wrapped in a gray-striped blanket. Louis turned the skiff about and hurried to the dock of the state trout hatchery, where he told the superintendent what they'd seen. 'Shorty' Immenroth laughed it off at first, said it was probably a deer. Nevertheless, he went out on the lake with Louis. There on the crystal-clear water, Shorty saw the outline of the object, a pure white shoulder showing through a tear in the blanket, and an alabaster foot dangling from one end of the bundle, a piece of rope tied around the ankle.

"It was a fact—she'd turned to soap. The lake is fed continuously by Olympic Mountains snowmelt. When you're six hundred feet down in frigid water, you don't rot. You're preserved, that's what, and saponification sets in. That's what it's called. Saponification. It means that after the cold stopped the decay, salts in her system changed all her fatty tissues little by little, and she turned to soap. She was down there for three years at forty-four degrees Fahrenheit, just exactly what the process required. Because the soap was lighter than the water, she came to the surface. The transformation must have happened to past corpses too; all of them must have turned to soap. So you might ask yourself, Penny, why only this one came to the surface, especially as she had been tied to something to weigh her down. There's more of a mystery there than people realize."

Her voice had lowered, and I found myself leaning forward, despite her smoky breath, eager as I was for her perceptions regarding the mystery. She paused and waved the cigarette about, evidently appreciating how she had put me at the edge of my seat. Then she took up her narrative again.

"Even after all that time in the depths, she was still recognizable as a strong, good-looking woman, her auburn hair hanging thick and wet. She was taken to a mortuary. The mortician and the cops found her to be as shapely as the day she was tossed in, not a speck of rot, a clean neutral smell coming off her. An elastic garter was still on one leg and she wore fragments of a green dress. As the soap was soft, she had undergone some damage when she was transported. Part of her face as well as her toes and fingers were gone or damaged.

"They put her in a potter's field grave. Fourteen months later the case broke, thanks to dental records distributed to five thousand dentists throughout the USA. A dentist of Faulkton, North Dakota, remembered the partial plate that had been kept as evidence. His records reminded him he'd made the plate for one Hallie Spraker. It didn't take long after that to find out who she'd married and that she'd disappeared from her Port Angeles residence on December 3, 1937. Hallie Illingsworth's fool husband must have known the day would come when his crime would be found out. He served nine years of a supposed life sentence before he was paroled, then disappeared, probably with an assumed name.

"All this is a matter of public record. But there's one

little piece of the puzzle still missing. That's the matter of the lake allowing her to return. When someone drowns in that lake, their corpse is never found. Never. So how did Hallie come back? Perhaps it's because the lake didn't kill her itself. It doesn't take offerings, it only takes lives."

I could tell by her manner that she had told me pretty much all she intended to, and her break from waitressing was done. As she stood, she told me, "There's an old geezer comes in here now and then, name of Benjamin White, lived in the area all his life. You should go and talk to him."

Benjamin was retired and a widower. The thing he liked best to do was fish. He'd been a fisherman since he was a child, when his father took him on outings to lakes and streams far and near. Yet Benjamin would not fish on Lake Crescent, though it was the nearest place and was famed for a unique species of trout. I sat in his living room, notepad on my lap, listening to his story.

"Those Klallams weren't stupid; they knew their business. It's a damn strange lake. I was fishing there once when I was a young man. I'd sooner be tarred and feathered than fish there again.

"I'd gone in the early hours, well before sun-up, to a place up near the Sledgehammer I'd had a feeling about. I remember it was the second morning after Independence Day. There'd been crowds along the beaches two days before, setting off firecrackers, hardly helpful to a fisherman. Now most of those people had left. The stragglers were asleep at their campsites. There was a sliver of a moon and a passel of stars for company. The lake was so quiet, I lay back with my line in the water and fell plum asleep right there in my boat. The next thing I knew, I was having the damnedest dream.

"I was walking on the bottom of the lake. Six hundred feet down, they say; there I was, just walking along light on my feet, easy as you please. I didn't feel wet or cold or anything but light-footed. It was hard to keep my feet on the bottom. Everything was glowing blue so that I could see perfectly well. There, all about me, were old skeletons, their skulls grinning as I strode by. Near some of the skeletons were arrowheads in little heaps, as though a couple centuries had made quivers and arrows dissolve, leaving only the flints. One skeleton had an antique pocket watch on a gold chain dangling amidst the ribcage.

"Then I came to a body that was standing straight up and was not at all decayed. It was a tall woman wrapped in a blanket. Her reddish hair was drifting in the water. She was weirdly beautiful as she looked straight at me with glimmering eyes. I could have sworn she was alive. She poked one arm out of a hole in the blanket and beckoned me near with a slow sweep of her arm. I went over to her and took her hand, but the fingers came off and mushed up in my grasp like a soaked hunk of Ivory soap. She looked sad about her hand and pulled her arm back inside the blanket."

Benjamin stopped then, wiping a hand across his face, and I saw amidst small liver spots that his hand had become moist with sweat. He cleared his throat, and for a moment I fretted that he might not tell me more, having already suppressed his emotions to the point of breaking.

"Then it seemed to me as though she was talking. The effort of speech caused one side of her perfect and perfectly white face to fall away from the skull. She commanded, 'Unbind the rope. Set me free.' Only then did I realize she was floating upright because one leg was tied to a concrete patio brick. I felt in my pockets and discovered I had my scaling knife with me. I bent down and sawed through the rope. As she floated upward and away from me, I heard her fading thoughts come back to me, offering a grateful sigh of thanks.

"At that moment I woke up in my boat, the morning sun warming my face. I was pretty well distressed about the dream. I tried to put it out of my mind as only a nightmare. Later that day, the Lady of Soap was found by a tourist. After that, I knew it was more than a dream. You'll not catch me on that lake again, nosireebob."

I finished up my research on the Soap Woman of Lake Crescent early in the afternoon at the newspaper morgue. There I saw a photo of Hallie Spraker Illingsworth. I was shocked by an uncanny resemblance, and the notice that she had worked in the Lake Crescent Lodge. I hurried back to the lodge and asked the bartender, "Is that auburn-haired waitress on duty tonight?"

"Who do you mean?" he asked.

"I talked to her yesterday while she was on her break. She didn't say her name."

"I'm afraid I don't know who you mean. There's no woman with auburn hair working here just now."

As he turned away to another customer, I sat at the bar nursing my Roy Rogers and pondering some of the things the nameless woman had said to me the day before. *She wants people to remember her.* I looked about the room. There was nothing unusual. Yet I could feel her presence, I was sure of it; there was a palpability in the shadows of the lodge—nothing frightening, but rather mocking, or even glad because the story was told.

Legend of the White Eagle Saloon

Penelope Pettiweather,
Seattle, Washington, USA

Jane Bradshaw,
Oundle, Northants,
England

My dear Jane,

Can you imagine a teetotaler like myself spending a whole evening in a tavern? I'm sure you can — if there's a ghostie or two involved. A little article clipped out of an Oregon paper and handed to me by a friend who knows of my interests. A week or so later I found myself heading down the coast to Portland. I arrived in the city in the afternoon, and, after registering at a favorite bed-and-breakfast, I spent most of the rest of the afternoon doing my usual library research. Then I headed off to one of Portland's oldest bars, the White Eagle Cafe and Saloon on North Russell Street.

The music for which the place is famed was not yet going on, as it was still rather early. So the place was a lot more conducive to conversation than it would have been with a band. Even so, I'm so much more comfortable in a haunted house than in any kind of bar, and I have no experience talking to bartenders. So I shyly took a seat at the far end of the bar and quietly sipped a tomato juice.

The place was all mahogany wood and surprisingly attractive. There were only a few people in the bar, a relatively young and attractive clientele, mostly reading books or newspapers and staying to their own few cubic feet of world. The place did have a comfortable atmosphere overall, and I imagined it must be one of the friendlier places when things were hopping. I nevertheless felt out of place because to my way of thinking, beer tastes like swamp water filtered through moldy bread, wine tastes like cherries left in a sunlit puddle to go sour, and Scotch tastes like cleaning fluid or paint remover. And I always suspected that if tequila was supposed to have a worm in it, then a grasshopper must have crickets and katydids.

When the bartender came down to my end of the bar to see if I needed a refill of tomato juice, I handed him one of those silly little cards you sent me for Christmas a couple years ago. You remember — the ones that say "Penelope Pettiweather, American Ghost Hunter" under a lovely dingbat of clipper ship. I still have some of them because I usually feel too silly handing them out. But this time it seemed an icebreaker. The bartender laughed and introduced himself as Chuck Hughs, proprietor. He has a wise, owlish look. I imagined him not running a bar day in and day out, but way out in the woods with a tent and a Coleman lantern and a dozen good books.

We talked for a while, and I took notes. Then he said, "There's someone you really should meet." He made a quick phone call, then he came back to where I was sitting and said, "We got lucky. Anne was home and says she needs something to do anyway."

"Who's Anne?" I asked.

"She owned the place in the '60s. Those two ghosts were hanging around here even back then!"

"So there really are two?" I inquired. We'd only been talking about a ghost called Sam, but the little article I'd read had indeed mentioned a second ghost.

"Yeah, Sam drank himself to death, near as I can figure, unless he shot himself in the head. His girl was named Rose. They lived upstairs in separate apartments back in the '20s or '30s. Some of the rooms still served as a brothel. I've heard Rose weeping in the early hours, after the rock bands go home and the place is shut up and quiet. I don't know if she killed herself or was killed by Sam, but when she starts sobbing, she sounds awfully unhappy about something."

Chuck wandered away to serve patrons, but it was still pretty slow, so he wandered back to where I was sitting. He picked up where he left off. "Yeah, it used to give me the creeps, but I've gotten used to it. This place was awfully violent back in those days, so what can you expect with a history like that. Do you know much about Russell Street? In the time of the clipper ships, it was lined with bars, flophouses, and brothels. Any time a ship anchored in port, sailors would flood onto the docks and straight for the night life on Russell. It must've been great! My own bar dates all the way to the turn of the century. It's just about all that's left of those days of glory."

He wandered off again to serve customers, and ended

up in a conversation with someone else. I sat alone for quite a while, scribbling in my notepad. Writing is a kind of "trance," for the whole world seems to disappear when I get to putting something down on paper. And due to my special sensitivity, I often find myself "connecting" with things otherworldly as I write. In a moment I had to let my pen lie flat on the pad. I closed my eyes, for I felt *something* that few people would ever detect behind the hum of the day.

"Goin' to sleep on me?"

I was startled back to mundane awareness. Chuck had returned, ready to pick up his tale anew. "You know what the most annoying part is? That old boozer Sam keeps snitching my tequila. He drinks nothing else, and lots of it. There's been many a time I'd be in the basement before opening, or after closing hours, and I'd see the tequila delivery bottle start to bubble. That meant someone was up here drawing some of the stuff. This has been happening for going on fourteen years. That's how long I've had the place. I finally learned it never does a lick of good to come running up the back stairs to try to catch who the hell is doing it. It could be Rose, but I think it's Sam. I tried switching the bottles around and I even changed the whole method of delivery. But he always finds the tequila. Doesn't like anything else. Not just a little glass, either; he just sucks it down. I mean, it's a pain in the ass that I have to pay for some dead bastard's binges!"

"You've never seen him materialize?" I asked, which seemed a natural enough conclusion if Chuck wasn't sure which ghost was doing it.

"But I've heard his voice. Kind of funny sounding,

doesn't make a lot of sense, just some mumbling drunkard who seems to be ticked off. And now and then, I hear the two shots upstairs—bang! bang! I don't know what it means. Killed Rose then himself I suppose, but maybe only Rose. Maybe only himself, but it'd be funny if *that* took two shots."

Anne Audry wandered in, and Chuck introduced us. He showed her my silly card, but she didn't laugh. Took it seriously. She could tell I was actually pretty serious about this kind of stuff. All the same, I was feeling a little light-headed, so I said, "What the heck, Chuck! Line me up another tomato juice!"

"One for me too, but put something in it," said Anne, parking herself on the stool next to mine. She said, "So, you're the famous ghost story writer?"

I hadn't heard any mention of my being a writer, only an investigator, so, feeling momentarily important, I asked, "You've heard of me?"

"Nope. Just going by what Russell told me on the phone."

"Oh," I said, the importance knocked out of me. "Russell said Sam and Rose have been around since the 1960s."

"A lot longer than that, you can well believe! I found Rose's number in an old phone book from the '30s. No one's sure if she was killed or what, but she really did live upstairs, that's for sure. Sam's for real, too. When I ran the place, his room was still padlocked. No one had been in there for decades. There was no key. That's just how spooked people were by the place. But I pried the padlock off and opened up the room. It was all dusty and cobwebby, just like in a scary movie, but I don't get the creeps easy. Sam's bed hadn't been made since he was carried out of there. His wallet was still on the dresser. Had a picture of an old man and an old woman in it, and some loose change, cool old coins, I still have 'em. His longjohns were in the middle of the floor. These few things amounted to all his worldly possessions."

Chuck put a drink down in front of Anne then leaned forward to hear the story again. She said, "I guess I roused him by opening up the place, because after that I often heard him walking back and forth quite a lot. One thing did spook me, though. I'd go up there sometimes, and I'd feel him put his hand on my shoulder. Brrr!"

The evening was getting busier, and the noise level rising. A band was setting up as Anne took me upstairs to see Sam's room. But as we walked by another room, I stopped, feeling a sudden chill up my back. I asked, "Was this Rose's room?"

"No one knows."

"What?" The band had started playing at a high volume, and the sound through the floor was so loud that I could not hear Anne.

"No one knows!" she said louder.

"I think this was her room!" I said. The music, or the *something*, surrounded me like a glove.

The room was presently used for storage. I entered, and immediately the sound of the band downstairs vanished. I looked around and could not see Anne. More surprising still, the boxes that had a moment before been stacked here and there were all gone. Instead, I was standing in a bedroom that seemed recently used. It was a tawdry place, with cheap feminine bric-a-brac everywhere, a dressing table, a gas lamp with a cracked red cover. The bed was a tall four-poster with a badly trumped-up "canopy" that was nothing but an old bedspread tied to the tops of the high posts.

There were a great many pillows and covers piled up all over the bed, so that at first I didn't realize there were people in that bed. Then I saw the pale, round rear end of a man. Under him was a woman, and she was gazing at me from underneath his bulk. She had a flapper's hairstyle and smeared makeup. I was immediately embarrassed, and was about to apologize for my unexpected intrusion, but in that moment I realized the woman was not looking at me at all. I doubt she knew I was there. A third party was entering the room, and, when the prostitute saw who it was, she looked terrified.

I wanted to turn to see him, but it as though I were swimming in molasses. My whole body turned slowly, slowly, slowly, until what came into the periphery of my vision was an upraised arm holding a pistol. Two shots rang out. Until then, I had not heard a thing—not the squeaking of the bed, not the intruder's footsteps, nothing. Just those two gunshots. The prostitute's client lurched backward from among piles of covers, then fell to the floor with blood gushing from two holes in his spine.

Rose was weeping hysterically, but other than the two reports of the pistol, I still could not hear a thing. Everything was totally silent. Sam moved to the bedside and threw the gun in Rose's lap. In his left hand he held a huge mug of what I took to be tequila. His right hand, now that it was free of the gun, clutched at his own heart. He staggered out of Rose's room, heading toward his own, where, I suspected, he was momentarily to die of acute alcoholism and a heart disease.

The next thing I knew, I was sitting at a table downstairs in the bar. Anne was pressing a moist towel to my forehead. The band wasn't playing, doubtless out of curiosity over the woman who had had to be carried down from upstairs. They probably thought I had drunk myself unconscious!

"She's coming 'round," said Chuck's familiar voice.

"You're not going to die on us, are you?" asked Anne.

"I'm all right," I said, getting my bearings. "I saw them. Sam killed Rose's client. Then I think he had a heart attack."

"You were out cold up there," said Anne. "Maybe you were dreaming."

"Maybe you and Chuck dreamed about them a bunch of times," I countered.

"Touché," said Chuck, laughing.

That evening, relaxing in my room at the bed-and-breakfast, I was finishing my notes while everything was still fresh in mind. Like so many of these hauntings, Jane, nothing ever comes together quite as fully as we'd like. And when it comes to ghostly reenactments, I sometimes wonder if the spirits themselves haven't sometimes gotten their own histories mixed up! But one thing I felt certain about—though don't ask me to explain why I think this. You see, I don't really believe Sam and Rose knew each other very well. Sam just brooded over her until he couldn't stand it. She barely knew he existed. I'm sure it all came as quite a surprise to her that the drunkard down the hall thought she was worth killing someone over.

I don't know how or when Rose died. I think she lived another ten years, for the things I saw in the room, and her hairstyle as well, were from the '20s, whereas Anne had found evidence that Rose lived there in the '30s. She may never have gotten over what happened, probably wept herself to death, or died of syphilis or poverty after being abandoned by an evil world once her minimal good looks were all used up.

The thing I learn over and over again, Jane, is that the world is full of pain. Yes, it's always been filled with pain, and it always will be filled with pain. I can only hope that folks like you and I, who investigate the darkest corners of this thing we call reality—I hope we've learned something by what we've seen. If we have, then when Lady Death comes with her final kiss, we'll go with less grief and misery than those who linger.

Love,
Penelope

Sarah, the Ghost of Georgetown Castle

Penelope Pettiweather,
Seattle, Washington, USA

Jane Bradshaw,
Oundle, Northants,
England

My dearest Jane,

When you encounter ghosts around England, I fancy your having the same range of emotional responses as do I while investigating ghosts of the Great Northwest. You and I live so far apart, and see each other so rarely, that it is easy to project oneself onto the other — but I do feel we have a great deal in common. I have re-learned an old lesson about the "one thing" that most defends us from malevolent darkness, and as usual, it has to do with my investigations of occult matters.

In historical Georgetown, there is a big, three-story, turreted mansion known as the Georgetown Castle, built in 1889. I phoned one of the two young men who lived there, for I had long wanted to investigate phenomena associated with the house. They were friendly young men, open to my desire for an interview. I went immediately to Georgetown.

Pat and Jay had been in the house only a few weeks when they first spied a shadow moving by the closet door. Pat was very animated when he told me, "Just out of the corner of my eye I saw something. I looked up, and there she was! — this old lady looking totally insane! My God, I tell you — she held one hand around her throat, like this —" he clutched his throat to illustrate " — and with her other hand she started hitting Jay, like this —" he jabbed the air with his fist to demonstrate.

The ghost, they explained, was a tall, slender, severe-looking woman with eyes like burning coal, her hair done up in a Victorian bun, and wearing a floor-length white dress. Floating behind her was a portrait of a swart Mediterranean man "whose appearance," said Jay, "has an unavoidable suggestion of malevolence."

"As I watched the ghost strangling itself and punching Jay," continued Pat, "I was thinking, 'Wait a minute! I'm not crazy! This can't be happening!' Then while she's flailing away at him, Jay all of a sudden says, 'Oh, you must be Sarah,' and just like that she disappeared!"

Jay added, "I've no idea why I called her Sarah. She had somehow informed me this was her name. Have you heard of that before?"

"Yes," I said, accepting the freshly steeped tea that Ray handed me in a dainty cup. I explained, "Ghosts commonly express incidental telepathy. Or a sensitive viewer's own intuition can be heightened by factors of thousands." Then I asked, "What do you know about the Castle's history?"

They explained that for many years before they moved in, the grand old Victorian mansion had been allowed to fall into decay. Neighbors told stories of it having been a bordello and gambling den in the Depression, and that ill-gotten monies were still hidden in the walls. It was a boarding house briefly, but failed because no boarder would stay more than a night. "Once," said Pat, "an Ouija board told previous owners in which wall gold was hidden. They tore out that wall only to have Ouija tell them to tear up another, and then another, until there were holes in all the walls — and that's pretty much the way the place remained when we bought it."

There was, of course, no gold, but only a mischievous Ouija.

Jay continued, "Many people claim to have seen Sarah, for she's not at all shy. She has appeared to our party guests, considerably spicing up our events. She once rummaged through the suitcases of a woman visiting Pat and I from Los Angeles. 'Who was that old lady going through my belongings?' she asked the following morning at breakfast, not having been told about the ghost."

Pat said, "Once I heard a window breaking, but no window was found broken. While investigating, I was assaulted on a staircase, and fled to find Jay, telling him excitedly that something had tried to strangle me. The weird thing is, I didn't think it was Sarah."

"Who, then?" I asked.

"It must have been a clue as to how she finally died. The sound of the shattered glass was someone breaking into the house one night. I think someone killed the mad old woman because of the belief that she had gold hidden about."

"I run a Pioneer Square art gallery," said Jay, "and Sarah took in interest in my own work. Whenever I was working on a painting, she would intrude and start posing for me. She was insistent in wanting me to do her portrait, perhaps as a mate for the sinister one that sometimes followed her about. When I complied with her wish, she was afterward considerably calmer."

"One day," said Jay, "an elderly woman paid us an unannounced visit. She just barged right in, and said she was the granddaughter of the man who had built the house. She wanted to see what we were doing to the place. Then she noticed the portrait I had done of Sarah, and exclaimed, 'That's my dead great aunt!'"

"She told us the story of Sarah," Pat continued. "In the '20s and '30s, Sarah's brother-in-law had taken over the mansion for his gambling operations and prostitution. His partner, a Spaniard, fell in love with Sarah, and sired a bastard by her. The Spaniard later killed the child and hid the corpse under the porch. He killed his partner, and reportedly hid a fortune on the premises. Sarah went crazy with anguish for her child, and, like her lover, eventually died a violent death."

"Since we learned her story, Sarah has appeared less often," said Ray.

"But," added Pat, "Every time we tell someone she's gone, something happens."

"Every time?" I inquired.

"That's right," said Ray, and both of them pointed to Sarah's portrait. Standing beneath it was the old woman herself, no longer strangling herself, but clasping her hands under her throat. Then she turned slowly about and, though seemingly unable to see where I was sitting, she gazed directly at the two young men with such tragedy in her features, as though she worried for them constantly. Then she faded from our sight, and I let out a long breath.

"She seems to be looking after our well being," said Jay. "We've come to be very fond of her, and do wish she wouldn't worry so much."

"Perhaps she has cause to worry," I suggested.

"How so?"

"Your experience on the staircase of being attacked. It's possible the murderous Spaniard lingers as well!"

Pat and Jay turned to one another, and winced. I had finished my tea, and, thanking them for their courtesies, I left. Those young men are aware that I have a certain skill at convincing unwanted ghosts to leave a place; and I do expect, one day, to be asked to do something about the murderer who follows Sarah in the form of a malevolent portrait. But as for Sarah, she has as much right to live in that house as they. She is, I think, as fortunate as any ghost can be, to have been "adopted" by veritable nephews.

One of the great enemies of Evil is Love, and for so long as Ray and Jay and Sarah love one another, all darker spirits are harmless. That's the lesson from which we can all learn.

Love,
Penelope

Fritz, the Gentle Ghost of Shaw Island

Penelope Pettiweather,
Seattle, Washington, USA

Jane Bradshaw,
Oundle, Northants,
England

Dear Jane,

I am always delighted to receive your letters, and your experience with the kirkyard ghost of that sad little child you called Joan was heart wrenching. By a coincidence, late this very morning Mrs. Byrne-Hurliphant dropped by to brag to me of a successful exorcism of an infant ghost. My overlarge friend swept into my home with all her layers of overdress wafting perfume, her stubby arms upraised and her fingers fluttering—I knew instantly that she had come to boast of something or another. And as I listened to her, I found myself filled with sadness for the little spirit and not terribly impressed by my friend's gleeful squashing of its presence. It's bad enough to have died of abuse. But then, from a sorrowful afterlife, "to be done battle," as my witchy friend put it, seems to me all the more wretchedly unnecessary.

The infant she spoke of could be heard weeping on certain holiday nights, but was otherwise rarely detected. It didn't sound to me like it was any great nuisance. But the new family in the house was very unsettled by it, and so called in the popular witch, who is often getting herself in the news with her overblown sensationalism, making all of us spirit-watchers look like eccentric buffoons. It has always been the philosophy of Mrs. Byrne-Hurliphant that every ghost must be disabused of its habits and squashed as swiftly as possible, no matter how innocuous it seems.

Ordinarily I might agree it is best to help any ghost "continue onward" to another plane than this one, where, one can hope, there is greater joy than lingering. But my witchy friend expresses rather too much exaggerated glee over her successes, and approaches every spirit as though it were a hateful thing. She and I remain friends because of our shared "sensitivity" to things otherworldly; but I must say, her approach is so heartless, I sometimes wonder why I tolerate her.

After she left, I found myself pondering ghosts that might well deserve welcome, who add spice to a dwelling, who have as much right as the living to possess a house. I remembered Fritz, the gentle ghost of Shaw Island.

Al and Lotte Wilding's waterfront farmhouse in Blind Bay on Shaw Island, in its comfortably rustic setting, was a comfort not only for them, but also for "a gentle little spirit" whom they affectionately called Fritz. When the Wildings put their house and forty acres up for sale in 1987, they cheerfully advertised the existence of the ghost—truly a sales point for the romantically inclined who are not made skittish by invisible housemates.

The Wildings dwelt in the farmhouse for nearly thirty years, though at first it was only a weekend retreat. The ghost was present from the beginning. Lotte said, "You just get used to someone else living there. Once you do that, it's no big deal." They believe the ghost is that of Fritz Lee, who died at the age of twenty-one in the 1918 flu epidemic. He is buried on the property, the equivalent of about a block away from the house.

When they first obtained the property, the Wildings found all of Fritz's school books in his upstairs room, together with letters to his mother. They owned the house one year when Al's uncle experienced an unseen presence in that room. At first he tried to dismiss what was happening, but after three uneasy nights, Al's uncle would never sleep in Fritz's room again. It was used as a storage room throughout the decades to follow.

Fritz's mischief was restricted to poltergeist activity. He never manifested visually. Due to the house having settled with age, the doors scraped the floors, and did not open easily. Nevertheless, doors would at times open with inexplicable ease when no one was near them.

The Wildings' fond acceptance of the spirit seemed to induce him to spare them any personal nuisance. For the most part he bothered only the guests to the house, who were more easily excited. Al, a retired police officer, once had two fellow officers and their wives at the farmhouse for a weekend. They slept in the living room. Awakened by strange footsteps, one of the officers drew his gun. But when the lights were turned on, there was no one there. In another incident, a friend of their daughter stayed overnight and was certain of a presence at the foot of her bed.

A ghost's tastes in music rarely changes from the time of death, and as you know, Jane, many stories are told of ghosts interfering with music they don't like. Fritz was of this kind. Once when the Wilding children were playing rock-and-roll on the radio, the station suddenly changed to softer music. They tuned their station back in, only to have the music change a second time. They set the radio on the table and tuned it once more, then sat and watched it. The dial didn't move. But the radio soon began to pick up the softer music of an earlier era.

Along the years, only once did Fritz behave aggressively. The Wildings' grown daughter, Juliana Barnes, had been staying with them for about two years, but the time came when she prepared to move out. Her leaving upset Fritz. Lotte said, "Juliana and I were alone in the house and I was helping her move. As I was walking down from upstairs—with Juliana in front of me—I was hit on the back with a pillow. I turned and said, 'It's not my fault she's leaving!' Juliana asked me at the time why I looked so strange, but I didn't tell her what had happened until later."

On that same day, pots and pans hanging on hooks were caused to sway and clang together. Juliana Barnes said, "I thought that was strange. Maybe it's true he didn't want me to leave." It struck me as quite sad and sweet that even from "the other side," a young ghost can get a painful crush on someone, and regret their parting.

Juliana once said, "It gives you a strange feeling to have so many of his possessions and know he's buried not far away." She had often felt his presence. Once while Juliana was vacuuming, the unseen Fritz tapped her on the shoulder. "I never felt it was a harmful ghost. Rather than being afraid, I always felt protected by it. It wasn't a mean spirit. But it didn't seem to like strangers."

Her husband Patrick Barnes doubted the ghost's existence. Whenever a wind blew open the yard gate, he'd say, "There goes Fritz!" But twenty-eight years of phenomena versus his joking skepticism—it's hard to discount the experiences of the whole of the Wilding family.

I must tell you, Jane, that if I was to hear of Mrs. Byrne-Hurliphant setting out to do away with gentle Fritz, I would be tempted to intervene, to talk the present tenants out of hiring her services. I know how hard it is for some people to tolerate a bit of darkness drifting among them, reminding them of their own mortality. But a little pity just might do us some good, and even the dead just want to be loved.

Yours dearly,
Penelope

Ogopogo

Penelope Pettiweather,
Kelowna, British Columbia,
Canada

Jane Bradshaw,
Oundle, Northants,
England

Dear Jane,

Finally, finally, finally, I have seen Leviathan!

Here I am lounging comfortably in a lovely "rustic cabin" styled but really very plush room of a bed-and-breakfast near eight-mile-long Lake Okanagan in Central British Columbia. I'm safe and warm between the sheets, propped up against three fat soft pillows. Nevertheless, I am still shaking with excitement, so, if my handwriting is a bit unsteady, forgive me. I just had to write to you right away, for I recall telling you in a letter quite some while back that for all the ghosts I have seen in my life, I had somehow never managed to catch sight of a sea-serpent or lake-monster.

Well, now I have!

It all started as a safe little camping expedition with my pup-tent, sleeping bag, and a lantern to read and write by at night. I was staying in a camp ground. It had running water, showers, a few other niceties, so things weren't exactly primitive. But surrounding this "tamed" woodland area is some of the wildest, most beautiful forests you can imagine.

I walked about all day and was truly overwhelmed by the forest's beauty. Come evening, I retired to my campsite to ruminate and cling to feelings of awe. In the morning a pleasant, middle-aged ranger named Jack Tobb came around to collect a smallish fee for the camping space. When he caught my name, wonder of wonders, he knew who I was. Seems he's quite a reader, and his ranger house is filled with books, including one or two of my own. He came back later in the afternoon and had me sign *Northwest Houses and Their Ghosts.* Then, it seems, he told everyone else at their campsites—there weren't many, happily enough—that I was a famous author. Little be it for me to correct the exaggeration of "famous"!

This resulted in my being visited, throughout the day, by various and sundry folks who wanted to share ghost-legends and uncanny events with me. Quite fun that was. By the white-gas light of my lantern, late into my second night, I was writing all of it down before I forgot anything.

I was scribbling away, propped up on my belly with scrap paper rustling under my pen. Then, all of a sudden a grizzled old face poked itself into my pup tent and liked to scare the pee out of me.

It was a years-scarred, stunningly beautiful old Indian woman with braids wrapped around her head. She said, "Twenty dollars, I'll show you N'ha'a'itk. Ten dollars now, ten when you see her."

"Pardon me? You'll show me what?"

"N'ha'a'itk. Mister Jack, he says you would pay me twenty dollars to see N'ha'a'itk."

"Right now? Who is this 'no-hat-trick'? A local ghost?"

"Not a ghost. N'ha'a'itk. White people call her Ogopogo. She's big, but she hides good. Only I can take you. Nobody else can find her for sure. I have a boat. It takes a while to get there. Bring your lantern and something to eat along the way. Ten dollars now."

Well, for ten dollars now and ten later, I wasn't going to pass up the opportunity of night-long adventure with an old Indian woman, whether or not I saw Ogopogo. When she said that name, I knew exactly what she meant, for Ogopogo is by far the best-known lake-monster in the region. I had spoken to several people about that serpent over the years, during various visits to British Columbia, but never before had anyone offered to show the beast to me for twenty dollars.

I turned my lantern on low to save the white gas, got into my trousers and shoes, put on a backpack with some odds and ends in it—dried fruit, two hastily made sandwiches in case my new friend wanted one, a flashlight, matches, knife, things like that—and gave my guide her "ten dollars now."

"My name's Penelope," I said, as we sauntered through the dark forest by the dim light of my lantern. She wore a long, heavy skirt and hiking boots. She was thin and tall and took such long strides, with such surety in the darkness, I was hard-pressed to keep up. Her beautiful face showed a great age—I never asked how old, but eighty wouldn't have surprised me—yet she was as spry as I was at twenty.

"I am Mary Beaver-Who-Knows-Something," she replied.

"What a great name!" I exclaimed, then felt silly, hearing my loud voice in the night of the still wilderness.

"I am the number-one fisherwoman," she said. "That's how I got my name. I know everything that's in this lake."

We came to the lakeside. There was a small boat half out of the water. In the darkness it looked modern, fiberglass, extremely clean and tidy, with a good deal of fishing gear under the seats and tied to the inner walls. I climbed in and Mary shoved the boat off. She hopped in and oared the boat into deeper water, then lowered the motor's blades and we were off at a steady, slow clip.

"We must go slow," said Mary Beaver-Who-Knows-Something. "There might be logs floating. I know all the logs, but they move about."

The moon was bright. I turned off my lantern to save the white gas. The boat's engine was surprisingly quiet, for Mary had it operating slowly. She piloted from the rear, the moonlight full in her upraised face.

"I know a little about Ogopogo," I said. "It was first reported in the 1870s, by a pioneer woman, I thing her name was Mrs. John Allison."

"N'ha'a'itk has been here longer than that. My great-grandmother told my grandmother who told my mother who told me where to see her for sure. Women see her more often than men, so I am not surprised a white woman saw her back then. But she was not the first woman to see N'ha'a'itk."

"No, of course not!" I said, a bit embarrassed. "Ogopogo—I mean, N'ha'a'itk—she really likes women most? That seems quite curious to me."

"She brings rain and fertility. She blesses women's wombs. She blessed my womb. I have three daughters still alive, and eight granddaughters, and a great many great-granddaughters. I am sad to say not many of them care about N'ha'a'itk. One granddaughter cares, and when I am gone, she will be the only one who knows the way to N'ha'a'itk's lair."

"Do you show people at night so they won't know the secret place in the daylight? Or does N'ha'a'itk only come out at night?"

"N'ha'a'itk does not prefer the daylight. She doesn't prefer the night. She prefers the time just as the sun gets ready to rise, for she likes the sound of birds. I don't mind if you remember the way to her lair, but it isn't easy for others to tell where it is, even if they have been there before. Still, it is not intentionally my secret. N'ha'a'itk owns this lake, not I. N'ha'a'itk welcomes everyone who honors her."

"I'm greatly interested in the idea that she likes women best," I said. I did wonder if the real reason women saw the serpent more than men was because the secret of the lair was held by women, and Mary tended to show the place only to women.

Mary told me the story of one man who had seen N'ha'a'itk. "Long ago, Tayee Timba'skt said, 'Why do only women see N'ha'a'itk? It's because women tell silly stories to each other and to children! There is no N'ha'a'itk!' So he went out in his canoe at dawn. He made a song of disbelief." Mary began to sing Chief

Timba'skt's song. "'Nah-ha-ah-ah, nah-ha-ah-ah, there is no N'ha'a'itk, N'ha'a'itk is old women's lies, nah-ha-ah-ah, nah-ha-ah-ah.'' But he never sang that song again, because N'ha'a'itk lifted her big tail out of the water and knocked the Tayee out of his canoe. But N'ha'a'itk never causes trouble to anyone who believes in her power."

I tried to dredge out of my memory some facts about this lake-monster. I knew that in 1925 the BC government actually had a plan to equip ferryboats on the Okanagan with devices to repel Ogopogo attacks! But they were talked out of it by the half of the people who said there was no Ogopogo, and by the other half who said Ogopogo never hurt anyone. Ferrymen worried, though, because of the numerous times they bumped against something mysterious — in places where the water was known to be two hundred feet deep!

In 1926 a music hall tune popular in England celebrated Ogopogo, so it would seem she has had an international celebrity. If you ever find the sheet music for it, Jane, I'd appreciate having a copy of that! The songwriter assumed Ogopogo was male, contrary to Mary Beaver-Who-Knows-Something's belief, and the song went in part:

I'm looking for Ogopogo
The bunny-hugging Ogopogo
His modder wuzza mutton
His fodder wuzza whale
I'm gonna put a little bit
Of salt upon his tail.

Well, Jane, when I go travelling about the Northwest, I usually bring a satchel with researched materials with me. So I was able to look at my little file of Okanagon lore after I had checked into this bed-and-breakfast. I am now able to fill you in on a few things that I could only vaguely recall as I was sliding through the night atop those black, moonlit waters.

Here, with my notes and newspaper clippings spread around me, I find there were fishermen in the early 1900s baiting huge hooks with slabs of meat, trying to catch Ogopogo. Once there was an attempt to dynamite Ogopogo and make her float to the surface like a dead fish. In 1946, a local orchard farmer shot Ogopogo, and citizen outrage was such that the attorney general issued a document interpreting the Fisheries Act that extended protection to Ogopogo. In essence there is now a special law assuring her continued prosperity.

Along the years there have been a vast number of witnesses to Ogopogo's existence. Sometimes cars park all along the highway, with gaping onlookers pointing at a fin, a hump of coil, or even the head darting along at the surface of the water. Among the witnesses who've gone on record are an Anglican clergyman, two doctors, businessmen from Calgary and Vancouver, an entire construction crew, startled passengers on Greyhound buses, two newspaper publishers...and far more. In July of 1955 Ernest Callas signed a sworn statement, describing a creature with fins along its back, greenish brown skin of armored texture, four distinct humps, and nearly forty feet in length. Others say it is seventy feet long, and still others that it is only fifteen feet—there may well be a family of them.

In June of 1976 two men fishing south of Fintry spied the serpent. One of them told a local paper, "We were three-hundred yards off shore. That darned thing was a hundred feet farther out, but the wake was so great it carried us nearly back to shore. It was blue-black and moved caterpillar-like in the water. Now I know for sure Ogopogo is not a myth."

In 1977, Lillian Vogelsang took her daughter to a lakeside park. "I turned around and there it was! It was making all kinds of contortions in the water. I saw five humps. It seemed to be digging or fishing and its humps were three feet out of the water. It must have been fifty feet long and was green and shiny. Its coat glistened and its humps were smooth. Then it sank down very slowly, like a submarine. By then I had grabbed my daughter out of the lake, and will never let her swim there again!"

Roy Patterson McClean, one-time publisher of the Kelowna *Daily Courier,* took his retirement and spent most of his time at his lakefront property. "One day I saw the ducks all stirred up about something. There were hundreds of ducks flapping about in the water and taking off like the Devil was after them. Then I saw three humps parallel to the shore. My first thought was there were three car tires out there. I watched for a minute and a half, then lost sight of it as it went farther out in the lake. I can hardly believe it even now, but there *is* something that lives down there."

Someone who would agree was Paul Pugliese, a worker on the old ferry system. At dusk on September 7, 1968, "I came down to the water and saw that thing coming up. What a sight! I thought, 'Oh my god!' It was forty feet long, dark green, and had a head like a horse."

The reports are like a litany. In 1949, a Doctor Underhill with a friend spotted *two* Ogopogoes. Harry and Betty Staines of Westback, on July, 1976, saw a thirty-foot black eel easing along at about eight miles an hour. Joe Davignon, a fisherman, saw a snake-like creature of the same length at the north end of the lake. Sam McDonald of Kelowna, another fisherman, said he saw a fifty foot creature with three humps out of the water which was momentarily very still, then took off at a high speed. Over the years there have been several organized Ogopogo hunts, and in summer of 1977 eighty divers working half-hour shifts attempted a complete sweep of the lake, to no avail.

There are several theories about the serpent, none I would credit. I like the one about a clutch of plesiosaur eggs fast-frozen in the glaciers, then deposited in the lake as the glacier was melting millions of years later. For myself, if I had to come up with any theories, mine is simply that there remain many creatures undiscovered by scientists. In fact, every single day another un-cataloged and unnamed creature becomes extinct somewhere in the world—even as you and I, Jane, go about our daily affairs. Some people do worry that the Ogopogo will become extinct before real physical evidence of her existence can be established. In the middle to late 1970s, Arleen Gaal, a leading Ogopogo authority, organized protests against the use of herbicides in the area, lest the poisons pose a threat to Ogopogo's continued survival.

Mary stopped her boat's engine. It was still very dark as she took up the oars. We were far from the shore, the trees barely visible in outline under stars. Mary said, "N'ha'a'itk doesn't like the motor. I will paddle near her lair. The water is very deep here. You can light your lantern, N'ha'a'itk may want to investigate the light, and you'll get a close look at her."

Not with some slight doubt about getting *too* close a look, I lit the lantern. I took out my flashlight as well. As Mary oared us along, I pointed the flashlight into the black waters. In a few more minutes Mary pulled the oars in and placed them near the walls of the boat.

"Should I throw out the anchor?" I asked. The boat's anchor was a chunk of cement molded in a large-sized coffee can.

"N'ha'a'itk wouldn't like that," said Mary. "The water's too deep anyway. I haven't that much rope for my anchor."

We waited. For some while there was only the sound of water lapping at the hull, of a distant owl whose voice carried well across the waters. We ate sandwiches and dried fruit, and talked a while about (of all things!) what would happen after California fell off into the sea.

After a while, Mary Beaver-Who-Knows-Something began to sing quietly in her elderly but very sweet voice. "Hah-ah-ha-ha, hah-ah-ha-ha, N'ha'a'itk is a pretty maiden, ha-ah, N'ha'a'itk is a strong matron, ha-ah, N'ha'a'itk is an old princess, ishi-nai, ishi-nai, hah-ah, ha-ah."

As she sang, birds on the distant shores joined in, providing a lovely counter-melody. I noticed that the eastern sky was ever so faintly aglow. Mary's song seemed to be on the order of an invitation.

The boat began to rock back and forth, not violently, but it was very noticeable. I was momentarily alarmed. Mary sat perfectly still, singing her song, which eased my worries. The rocking became more pronounced, and the water all around the boat appeared disturbed in some curious manner. There were not exactly waves, but a whirling disruption. I realized the boat was turning around, counter-clockwise. This continued as the sky lightened from darkest indigo, becoming paler and paler by the minute

Around and around the boat turned slowly, slowly, until finally the disruption from below stopped and the boat eased itself still.

Mary stopped her song. I looked her right in the face, and there was such serenity there that I, too, felt only serenity. The shoreline's bird population was now a great chorus indeed. I was absorbed in that sound, expecting nothing more of my night's adventure, needing nothing more to count it a success.

I had been awake the whole night, but felt more relaxed than drowsy. When I was my most at peace, one serpentine loop and then another and then another arose from the lake. The creature was less than thirty feet off the bow, and appeared to be twenty or thirty feet long even with most of itself submerged. A fourth loop arose and I had just about decided that the tail must be only ten feet away from the boat, just under the surface of the water.

I had guessed wrong. It was the *head* that was nearest the boat. N'ha'a'itk raised her head straight up out of the water! She gazed at the vulnerable little boat, or at my lantern in the boat.

N'ha'a'itk had a distinctly *mammalian* face — somewhere between a seal and baby lamb, but far bigger and broader. The dark, moist eyes were now focused entirely upon me, as mine were upon her. The lamplight went out—it was out of white gas—and still the gleam remained in N'ha'a'itk's eyes. There was *wisdom* in those eyes, though I'm sure I only project.

Less than three minutes passed, but it felt like hours. The sun arose, and N'ha'a'itk sank back into the water. Mary and I sat quietly for a long time. I felt we were really communing together. We communed with the wholeness of the earth. Something mystically important had happened.

I think Mary understood how impressed I was, how glad I was that she had invited me to this place, how I never would forget this night; or her singing with the birds; or the rising sun; or the visit from N'ha'a'itk. She smiled at me with grandmotherly tenderness.

Then she put an open hand toward me, smiled with extraordinary sweetness, and said, "Ten dollars please."

Love,
Penelope

Harmless Ghosts

"Truth be told, my dear Penelope, I *do* believe in ghosts. Yet you will forgive me for saying I have doubts about some of the stories chronicled in your various books and articles."

I must say I was stunned by Jerome's confession. I had known him for years and thought him an utter skeptic. He loved to cast aspersions on what I, whether eccentrically or not, consider my life's work. And I've never demanded that all my friends support me in endeavors they find peculiar. But here I was finding out that Jerome had never been a skeptic in the least. The many times he "pshawed" my chronicles of supernatural events, he was really doubting my personal integrity.

"Jerome," I ventured, "do you realize what you have just said to me?"

"Yes, that I don't believe any of those silly stories you have written down for that antiquary's journal in England, much less those big books you've done about modern hauntings."

"Yet you do believe in ghosts."

"Yes I do. I have an acquaintance, a relative you might say, who lived in a haunted apartment building. I had something to do with resolving that particular mystery. The resolution was quite simply the identity of the ghost, who my relative could not possibly have known anything about. So I'm not a doubter as far as that goes, although I've never personally made the acquaintance of any such creature."

"Forgive me if I seem affronted," I said, sounding only half as annoyed as I felt inside. "So ghosts are real — it's *my* ghosts which are fabrications. Why have you chosen this moment to inform me that you consider one of your closest friends an outright fraud?"

Jerome's animated and much-creased expression went suddenly pale. "I meant no insult at all!" he exclaimed. "I thought we were good enough friends that I could tell you an honest feeling."

"As indeed we are," I allowed. "And I have never minded your treating me as though you thought me prematurely dotty and a superstitious eccentric. But your honest thought, it turns out, is that your good friend Penelope Pettiweather spits untruths left and right."

"That wasn't my thought at all! I don't doubt you believe everything that you say you believe."

"Then, dear friend, you are calling me mad."

"A bit angry, I gather, but not mad," he said, trying feebly to inject a moment of amusement into our conversation. I did not feel ameliorated. He ventured further. "You say that you are sensitive to the occult world, and I believe you are. But isn't it possible that, once in the vicinity of such creatures as my very own relative witnessed, you become somewhat excitable on account of your sensitivity, and enlarge upon the experience in a manner calculated to heighten the effect?"

"Calculated, you say?"

"Only subconsciously, Penelope. I don't mean you're trying to fool people—only yourself."

I could not for the life of me tell what he was getting at. He didn't think me either mad or a liar. But he did think I made things up without realizing it. This was patently absurd to me, and I felt no less insulted. "I must say," I began, "you express yourself badly. You say I'm not a liar but have told tales which cannot be true. You say I'm not mad but have experienced things that could not have happened."

"Yes, that's right. You've got it." He was more satisfied than I with my rephrasing of his opinion. He continued. "You see, while ghosts surely exist for some reason or another, there's no reason to suppose them in any manner malicious. Yet the books and articles you have written, many about personal experiences, all have a foreboding tone to them, if not an absolutely menacing character. But this cannot be right. Why, I'm certain that ghosts are nothing but lingering aspects of our own selves. Even someone with a bad character can only be an insubstantial, utterly helpless shade. And shadows, my dear Penelope, do not bite."

"I see," said I, thinking I was beginning to understand his belief. "Despite the fact that you have never seen me in a temper, or suffering from the vapors, or getting excited in any untoward manner, yet you believe that I have an excessive and unjustifiable response to mere shadows."

"That's it. The shadows may indeed be *something*. But that something is harmless. Just as some people are instantly terrified and have an unreasoning sense of doom at the sight of an itty-bitty spider or some old tomcat, you, Penelope, have a phobia for ghosts, all the more tragic for your affinity or sensitivity to their existence."

"And you feel you have empirical evidence as to the harmlessness of supernatural events?"

"My friend's ghost, yes."

"Friend is it, or relative?" I asked. "You're a bit vague on that point, Jerome. I for one never draw sweeping conclusions without the specifics."

Now it was Jerome's turn to be embarrassed. He'd gone pale when he realized he'd insulted me. Now he became red-faced because I'd tripped him up in, at least, a mild untruth. "All right," he said. "I hate to carry tales about my own dear mother, rest her soul, and it has been my habit to tell the story as having happened to 'a friend' or 'a relative.' But yes, it was my own mother, though I entreat you not to think she was any kind of fool or madwoman to see a ghost."

"Since only fools and madwomen generally see them?" I said with a rueful expression.

"No, no! Not that! Oh, dear, I do offend you today, don't I? Well, let me tell it quickly, so you'll know what I mean. My mother and her second husband—my father had been dead for years, and I anything but a young man—moved into an old apartment building near Everett. This must have been, oh, twenty years ago. Bill—he was my stepfather, but as I was a grown man at the time I tended to just think of him as a friend and my mother's husband—was an antique wholesaler often traveling about making 'finds.' So my mother was commonly alone. She had been a widow long enough before her second marriage, she didn't mind the weeks Bill was gone. But the apartment bothered her for some reason and she frequently called to have me stay over. It was some while before she told me there was a ghost. Of course I laughed at that. I'd stayed with her numerous times and never seen a thing.

"She told me that the ghost sometimes turned on the bathtub tap in the middle of the night, opened doors, and now and then moved things about to suit herself. The ghost was an old woman. My mother claimed to have seen such things as the overstuffed chair sink in, as though an invisible person had sat down. And on various occasions, the old woman would appear, especially in the kitchen. The odd thing was that the old woman would be floating about four inches above the floor, generally in front of the stove; and she would be making a stirring motion as though there were a pot of bubbling stew. It quite unnerved my mother.

"My mother's sense of honesty was so extreme that I often thought it was a fault rather than a virtue. If someone's hair looked awful though it had just been done, and that someone asked, 'How do you like my hair?' she was apt to say, 'It looks dreadful and your hairdresser should be stuffed.' No tact, my mother; but honesty was her obsession. So I believed she had seen what she said she'd seen. But without corroboration, I had to admit to her that I feared she was suffering from delusions. She was getting on in years herself and probably thinking so much about becoming a senior citizen that she had begun to imagine an even older woman in the apartment with her.

"Mother insisted it was no such thing. She added that

on two occasions she had actually spoken with the ghost. 'This is my home and I want you to get out,' she told the ghost. And the translucent old woman drifting above the floor replied, 'It was my home first and you should leave.' My mother felt mildly threatened by this and started having me stay with her quite a lot, when Bill was away.

"I asked around about a tenant who might have worn black slacks and black sequin blouse, of a sort popular in the late 1940s; who was stout and had short, tightly curled white hair and rather too much makeup in the wrong places. This was as my mother described the ghost. Nobody had heard of such a woman having lived there. But the fellow who owned the apartment was a senile goat in a nursing home. His children managed the apartment house. I went to see him and it was hard going but I made him understand what I wanted to know.

"He said a lady named Eppy Sarton had died in that room in 1953, wearing her 'night out' clothes, including a black sequin blouse. As she was old and half blind, it was true she put on rather too much makeup in odd places. But she was otherwise pretty healthy and her death had been a surprise to everyone. An unexpected stroke.

"After that, I looked up the Everett Sartons, and found a great-niece of Eppy Sarton who had some pictures of her great-aunt. I borrowed one faded photograph to show my mother. It was exactly the woman my mother had been seeing. So, I knew I had the corroboration I needed, the evidence! I had to admit my mother was by no measure demented and that such a thing as a revenant does exist!"

When Jerome had finished telling me his mother's ghost story, he looked perfectly satisfied that I would no longer be miffed.

"But this does not explain," I said evenly, "why you confess such a wholehearted doubt of my own experiences!"

"Why, don't you see…" he was getting animated again "…the old woman's ghost was absolutely harmless! In fact, once my mother was able to call it Mrs. Sarton, it stopped troubling her at all. Oh! There was one more thing. I looked at some blueprints kept by the city of Everett and established that the apartment house had been completely renovated in the late 1950s. The floors had been higher originally, the ceilings vaulted. That was all changed. The ceilings were lowered. An extra floor was gotten out of it. That's why the ghost of Mrs. Sarton appeared to walk above the present floor. Fit very neatly, I thought! But every bit of it, harmless as can be. Yet have you ever seen a harmless ghost, I good friend Penelope?"

"Certainly," I said, still quite annoyed.

"Well, perhaps you have; but aren't most of them malevolent? I've read your books and they're always scary stories. Not like a real ghost at all."

"My dear Jerome," I said, my voice strained. "As well to say that since George Washington was a fine leader for his country, then surely there was nothing wrong with Hitler. But to be frank with you, ghosts are trouble wherever they appear, to one degree or another. And if your mother was never harmed in any manner, she was rather luckier than you may realize."

"See! Just as I thought! You always find a malevolence in things! Absolutely no reason for that, Penny. Except for the drama, of course. My mother's ghost would make a pretty boring chapter for one of your books, unless it had bitten off some of her fingers or something like that."

He was referring to the Maynard Ghost I had written about. It bit off some poor child's fingers before it could be gotten rid of. The smug look on Jerome's face was an extraordinary annoyance to me! Did he think young Jenny Maynard bit off her own fingers and spirited them away without trace before her parents got her out of that room? I shook my head in dismay and said to Jerome:

"Did your mother die peacefully?"

"Isn't that a change of topic?" he said.

"Only if she died peacefully. I seem to recollect your mentioning she died of a broken neck, poor old gal."

"Well she was getting feeble by then. Shouldn't have been in a second floor apartment, I suppose. I'm rather glad I didn't find her at the foot of the stairs. It was Bill found her, poor fellow. He really loved my mother. But what is this you're suggesting? That my mother was *pushed* by a ghost? I won't stand for that, Penelope! Getting morbid where my mother is concerned! You have absolutely no reason to presume such a thing."

"You're right, and I would not venture to say it happened that way at all, Jerome. At least, not until I could correlate some dates and interview some neighbors."

"What an insidious seed to plant in my mind, Penny! It's not a coincidence that escaped my notice. I had found the exact date of Mrs. Sarton's death. It was May

22, 1953. My mother slipped and fell down those stairs on a May 22, also. I do say, though, that this is exactly the kind of meaningless coincidence that you are capable of running wild with!"

"If you will read my books more carefully, you'll know that I only heed coincidences when they begin to pile up. For instance, what were the ages of Mrs. Sarton and your mother the day of their deaths? Well, you don't know that one yourself. I venture you'll be checking the newspaper morgue tomorrow. Don't be too surprised by it. Your methods of detection in tracking down the ghost's identity were very impressive, Jerome, so you must have asked yourself some other questions later on: Had your mother been especially anxious during the days before the accident? Did she disagree with you that Mrs. Sarton was a harmless spirit? Did you talk your mother into taking no precautions? Do you call me variously a fool, a liar, an imaginative hysteric, and so on, because it hides your own guilty feelings in having reassured your mother a ghost was only a harmless shadow?"

Jerome was awash with sweat. He stood quickly, fists clenched, though I was not afraid of him one bit. He stammered, "The dead can't hurt anyone! I tell you that!"

"Very well, Jerome. You may be right," I said, trying to calm him. I really hadn't meant to hit his sore spot so firmly. I wouldn't have said anything but that he'd piqued me with unintentional insults the whole afternoon. He sat down, removed a handkerchief from a pocket and mopped his brow. He said, "You won't write about this one, will you?"

...Penelope Pettiweather, Ghost Hunter / 115

"I should think not," I said. "I never investigated it. I don't write about hearsay—and it was your mother's adventure, not yours."

He sank into himself, looking unhappy. "I did tell her it would be silly to worry Bill or to trouble everyone by moving out. It *was* my fault, wasn't it, Penelope? I made an awful error. I always knew it! I practically killed her myself!"

"Don't excite yourself, Jerome," I said. "I wish I'd understood your mind a couple minutes sooner. I wouldn't have teased you as severely. Your mother was old, after all. If it hadn't been a quick death with a broken neck, it might have been a slow and awful one with strokes and a failing mind. Sometimes the only thing we can do is think of a tragedy as a blessing in disguise. Do that for me, Jerome. And if tales of evil spirits upset you, do you and me both a favor. Don't read my books from now on."

The Burnley School Ghost

"Penelope," said my host, setting his teacup on the side table by his armchair, "as you are such an expert on the paranormal, what can you tell me of the old Burnley School ghost here on Capitol Hill?"

Herbert was a retired city planner and a friend for two decades. It seemed to me he'd always been old, and now that he was beginning to get feeble, I tried to visit him at least twice a month. He doesn't ordinarily share my enthusiasm for the supernatural, so I was surprised by his query. "What has piqued your interest in that old haunting?" I asked.

"Well, nowadays there's a language lab where the art school used to be, and my granddaughter works there. She knew nothing of the building's past history, yet just the other day she mentioned how spooky the place was especially if she stayed to work after hours. I told her I remembered hearing tales of that building even when I was a lad, but I couldn't recall particulars for her."

"As it happens," I said, "I have some personal experience with that particular spirit. There have been so many reports about it over the years, but things quieted down a bit in the 1980s, so when in 1991 I visited the dental clinic that was at that time using the main floor of the building, no one really knew of the old tradition. Even so, they knew perfectly well that the place was haunted! They were so relieved to have me show up to reassure them they were not all crazy — and they actually allowed me to spend a night alone in the basement."

"Good lord, Penelope!" Herbert had reached for his tea and nearly spilled it. He exclaimed, "Whatever possesses you to such experiments!"

"I was a cat in a former life," I jested.

"Well, don't keep me in suspense, Penelope. I can see you're dying to spin the tale out for me."

And that I did.

The Burnley Ghost dwells in the century-old Booth Building at East Pine Street and Broadway on Seattle's Capitol Hill. The building itself has something of a history. President Taft visited it in 1909, when a large auditorium was used for ballet and piano recitals. It was later used by the Entre Nous Dance Club of Broadway High School, and still later that upper floor was used as the high school's auxiliary gymnasium. There are a few years tucked between these uses when things are a bit uncertain, causing legends to arise regarding less wholesome purposes to which the building was subjected. Some say, for instance, that the Dance Club degenerated into a "roaring twenties" dance hall replete with brawls, illegal booze, and prostitution.

In 1946 the entire third floor of the building was leased by Edwin Burnley, a local artist, for use by the Burnley School of Professional Art, which in 1959 was taken over by one of Edwin's students, Jess Cauthorn, a well known water colorist. Leading Northwest artist Mark Toby had his studio at the school, and many other well-known artists and designers either graduated from or taught at the Burnley school.

In 1967, Jesse Cauthorn told the late psychic investigator Susy Smith that he had often heard an invisible presence late at night. When no one else was in the building, he heard desks being shoved about behind closed doors, or doors slamming on the third floor. Cauthorn's student John R. Nelson heard the ghost ascending the back stairway. Often when John was working late on large art projects, the sound of the ghost on the stair arrived between eleven o'clock and three in the morning. He said, "New students don't believe it, of course. But after they've had occasion to work late at night, then they change their tune." One student, Jennie Millar, admitted, "I went bellowing down the hall. I was all alone and I wanted to run out, but I was too scared to go down the stairs." Ellen Pearce, who had a studio on the notorious third floor, heard the ghost moaning in the darkness, but when the lights were turned on, there was no one visible. Several other students interviewed by Suzy told similar tales.

As late as 1981, Jess Cauthorn's daughter, Nan, at the time a twenty-seven year old commercial artist, kept an office in the Burnley School. Nan often worked late. She told local news reporter George Foster, "I'd swear I heard someone coming, and I'd go out to see who it was, and there'd be nobody there. It gets to a point where it's almost annoying."

Then there was Mary Renick, a young office worker and Burnley School student. She, too, heard someone in an empty hall one night when working late. "I poked my head out in the hall and couldn't see anybody. But there were those footsteps going down the hall right in front of me. I flew down the stairs and out the front door." She thereafter wore a cross on her necklace when spending evenings at Burnley. These accounts are the tip of the iceberg; there are dozens of like reports.

Rumor was that the ghost was an eighteen-year-old high school student who died violently on the premises, but no one was able to say what his name was, for the specific incident, if true, was lost to all but the vagaries of folk memory. Broadway High School had once been directly across the street from the Booth Building. The High School had previously rented the very space that subsequently became the Burnley Art School for use as a makeshift gymnasium. News reporter Paul Andrews in 1983 re-investigated the story, and was informed that the ghost was a youth killed in a fight during or immediately after a basketball game. He was knocked down a flight of stairs and broke his back. This agreed with Nan Cauthorn's sentiment that the ghost just wanted to play basketball, and was annoyed that the third floor was no longer a gymnasium. She said, "That's why he keeps moving things around."

When the academy was bought out by an East Coast firm, it was renamed Seattle Art Institute, and changed its address shortly after. Without the influx of baffled students and late-night workers, one would expect the reports of the ghost to come to a close. Today the space occupied by the Burnley School is used by the Seattle Central Institute of English. The building closes at six; rarely is anyone there past seven. The second and third floors are all remodeled and modernized. There is no longer much of an opportunity for anyone to perceive the spirit during his nocturnal perambulations. Even so, a reporter in 1987 spoke with Isbel Trejo-Conner, manager of the microcomputer lab on the second floor, who stated the ghost had taken to bothering chiefly young women. One day she was in the storage room taking inventory when a shelf of software seemed to "leap" across the room and pelted her in the head. This happened again a few days later, but Isbel, annoyed, yelled at the ghost and he never bothered her again.

Having completed archival research and a few phone calls, I felt I knew sufficiently about the ghost to investigate the premises myself, if I could gain access. The supernatural can be a dangerous thing to poke around in, but things are far less apt to turn out badly if approached with a little understanding of the events, of the ghost's motivations, and so on.

There were certainly many unresolved threads, but this is usually the case with the paranormal. Such things are rarely easily pigeonholed, as there is ultimately very little about "the other side" that we can grasp with absolute certainty. Still, it is my usual procedure to find out all I can about a ghost before I try to make personal contact. They tend to be quite placid and harmless if you know in a general way what they're up to; but they can become unpredictable and even dangerous if they're approached without any sense of what has caused them to linger.

It seemed to me that in this case, the ghost's long history adhered to a perceived pattern of minor annoyances. It was a rather obnoxious but not a malicious ghost. He, or it, had never attempted to harm anyone.

While it is not wise to take too much for granted in these things, I nevertheless felt that this was one case which I could expect to be a particularly strong haunting, but with none of the sort of thing I'd have to "be on guard" about.

Someday it will really sink in that I should never be too certain of anything!

There were indications that renovations to the building had driven the ghost into the unaltered basement of the Booth Building, or that he retired there during daylight hours. The slain youth apparently continue to haunt the basement under dental offices that took up the main floor previously occupied by a Savings and Loan. Cindy, a dental assistant, informed me the ghost was still felt, but that clinic workers are mostly afraid to speak of it. She personally will not work in the building alone in the evenings, because of the uneasy feeling of the place.

When I showed up for on-premises investigation, no one at the clinic knew that for several decades the Burnley ghost was extremely well known, nor was the name of "Burnley" any longer remembered by the dental office workers. The current manifestations are quite different from the older reports, as though it requires an oral tradition to "sustain" a certain style and type of haunting. This, I think, is an important feature. Traditions can be lost and never recovered, but a location genuinely suffering from otherworldly exposure will invoke eerie emotions even among those living who have no knowledge of the folklore that previously shaped the haunting but, perhaps, shapes it no longer.

The dental workers did provide independent

confirmation of a continuing presence of some kind. That it had changed markedly should have set up warning bells, but in this case my archival research had put me off guard, and I had really decided that there was nothing untoward about the Burnley ghost except that an unusually large number of people had experienced its presence over a fairly long period of time.

The tradition of the ghost being someone who fell down a staircase faintly persisted. Office workers admitted they had heard something along that order from an elderly dental patient who knew a bit of the building's history. And there was an additional theory or rumor regarding the ghost's origin. It is presently understood that the third floor of the building had once been a dance hall. It gained a reputation for violence and prostitution. One evening, someone was thrown to his death from an upper story window. It might be true that a seedy dance hall used the space, or this may be an imperfect folk-memory of the high school dance club that used the space long before World War One.

It was in any case rather thrilling to ascertain that the Burnley Ghost was at minimum in its seventh or eighth decade of uninterrupted haunting. It had, if anything, increased in potency and weirdness. The most extraordinary manifestation at the old Booth Building, which I was informed took place in 1988, has got to be one of the strangest and most unique of all Northwest phenomena.

Cindy introduced me to a young Korean worker at the clinic, who I will call by the likely name of Lee, which is not his name, as he wishes anonymity. All around his office he had mounted mirrors at various angles, and was so extremely shy of speaking of his experience that I nearly despaired of obtaining the story. The mirrors were arranged in just such a manner that nothing could sneak up on him.

"No, no," he said adamantly, turning in his chair to face away from me. "I can't talk about that."

"But Cindy said you saw something in the basement."

"No, no, if I talk about it, it will come."

He believed ghosts disliked mirrors, which I've discovered is sometimes true. Lee's belief in the protective merits of mirrors was an extension of the Asian belief that ghosts will not cross water. It also allowed him, quite simply, to always know what was behind him. He was not a cowardly man, but when it came to the supernatural, he fretted about inviting trouble. He could not be convinced by any argument to go into the basement with me, to show me exactly where he had once had a frightening experience. I assured him of the ghost's long history as a harmless nuisance, but Lee would have none of it.

"You don't know!" he said, convinced of its malignancy.

At length I pried loose part of the story, but Cindy had to fill in the details for me when Lee reverted to his unwillingness to draw references between himself and the spirit. It seems Lee had gone into the basement for something or another, and discovered a deluge pouring from the ceiling. He hurried back upstairs to tell the office manager to call a plumber and the building's owner, for a pipe in the basement ceiling had burst. The manager and Lee grabbed as many rags and towels as they could find and went into the basement to try to sop up the water even as it continued to poor forth from the ceiling. Finding the task hopeless, they returned to their duties in the clinic and awaited the owner and the plumber.

The owner and plumber arrived in short order. Everyone went directly into the basement, where the floor was completely dry. There was no evidence of water ever having issued from the ceiling.

It was impossible to know what to make of the phantom waterfall in the basement, except that a ghost so long positioned may have developed an imagination of its own. Ghosts crave attention, and for a long time the Burnley Ghost was all but forgotten.

On the other hand, it was conceivable that the ghost had never been a young basketball player at all, let alone a victim of murder tossed from a window, nor even a ghost as we commonly think of them. This was merely how the presence came to be perceived during the Burnley School years, for it does seem that the supernatural can be reshaped by human expectation. Lee may have seen the entity in something closer to its true form, a water-spirit who was long ago honored by the native population as the divinity of a well or stream. Its troublemaking through the Burnley School years came about for want of its ancient worshippers.

Cindy asked me if I'd like to see the basement, and of course I was eager. My prying about was allowed because "when the boss is away, the mice will play." But about then the boss returned. I was asked in hushed whispers to return the following evening after closing, and Cindy would let me in. She said, "There's a basement exit door. I can lock up the clinic and leave you in the basement, and when you're ready to go, just make sure the basement door is locked as you leave."

So my raison d'être was upon me. Face to face with a spirit! Alone in a spooky basement by night! Oh boy, was I ready!

But I must add that I was not without some slight qualms. In my researches I have found that ghosts are generally "lost" for some reason or another, and if you can discover what the thing is that makes them linger, you can exert a degree of authority over them. They can even be politely, gently "exorcised" if you know what they're seeking. So, had the ghost really been a basketball player, and had it been dangerous (which, it seemed to me, it was not), then to bring a basketball with me would "placate" it. I might even be able to communicate with it when it found I would not flee from its presence.

Therefore, the next day, I dropped in at a sporting goods store and bought a basketball, as a tentative offering to the ghost. It had never spoken to anyone previously, but then no one except a fraudulent, crackpot medium who assisted my fellow psychic investigator, the late Susy Smith, had ever tried. Certainly this would be the first time anyone had ever offered it something it wanted.

Unfortunately, I was beginning to think that the haunting was something more on the order of an "elemental." It might be very ancient indeed, and the basketball would mean nothing to it, despite the extant lore. Then again, if I was confronting a brawler who was tossed from a window, the basketball might again prove to be a misguided offering, and the ghost would become angry.

While I hated to admit it, Lee was not entirely deluded about the need to be careful around these things. Ghosts can be quite startling but nine times in ten they're perfectly harmless; by contrast, elementals are for the most part not to be trifled with. They brood about the days when they were honored as gods, or feared as demons, and placated with ceremonies and sacrifices. In our modern age, they feel deprived. They are often strikingly powerful given ideal circumstances for them to reveal themselves.

Nevertheless, I elected to believe in the harmlessness suggested by this ghost's history on the third floor, and blindly overlooked the possibility that this water-spirit, differently located in the basement, might well express itself without benevolence.

Mine is a hobby wherein simple assumptions can prove thrillingly mistaken!

There are a couple of things that happen to those of us who delight in tinkering about at the periphery of the Unseen. The first thing is that we for the most part lose our fear of things that just might be, upon occasion, wisely feared. The second thing is that we become just a tad bit bored with the predictability of the majority of ghosts—those which flit about from room to room without much purpose or resolve.

So, although the news of the phantom waterfall sent icy chills up my spine which I should have taken as a warning from my subconscious, I was at the same time barely able to restrain myself from clapping my hands with delight over the promise of novelty.

And in the manifestation's favor, I must say it was one of the most beautiful spirits I would ever see.

Cindy locked me in the basement before she closed the clinic and went home. I was absolutely alone. The basement was relatively well lit by an electric bulb on the ceiling. I had brought a book, since it was still early in the evening, and from my research I believed the likeliest hours of the haunting would be between eleven and three in the morning.

I sat under the incandescent light on a somewhat rickety swivel chair that had been relegated to the basement because it was half broken. On the floor between my feet sat the basketball like the world's biggest Florida orange. I was reading an ornate antique edition — the only edition — of Leon Mead's Victorian anthology *The Bow Legged Ghost and Other Stories* and chortling to myself from time to time, the articles being predominantly humorous.

I lost track of time. It was a big collection of stories and essays, so hours passed like minutes as I read. In the middle of a giggle, I thought I heard an odd tinkling halfway between Christmas bells and a rushing stream. I became very still, setting my book on one of the basement file cabinets. I listened. Far, far away I distinctly heard a rill or stream babbling over stones.

It was a musical sound, very pretty, but so faint it might well be chalked up to imagination. As I concentrated, it began to sound a bit like a multitude of sweetly piping voices, almost laughter. And as I closed my eyes to better concentrate, the piping became a lilt, having about itself a tone of irony or even disdain.

Directly in front of me, a single drop of water fell from the ceiling. I looked up and was somewhat blinded by the incandescence of the bulb. It appeared, impossibly, that the water-drop had fallen from out of the bulb. As I was watching, there began, all at once, a thin continuous stream of water from the bottom of the bulb! It did not short out the electricity, which was evidence in itself that the manifestation was spiritual.

I put my finger into the stream. It felt decidedly wet. As I looked at my moistened finger, there seemed no reason to doubt it was anything but ordinary water. Yet as I watched, it evaporated with exceeding rapidity, despite the humidity in the basement. In a split second, my finger was chilled and dry.

Water was puddling around my shoes. The orange basketball rocked to one side as water gathered about it. The descending stream was widening. I stood from the swivel chair to get out of the way of falling water when, with an instantaneous suddenness, the stream burst downward as a curtain about three feet wide.

The water spewed down with such force that I was soaked in an instant. I was thrust backward into the swivel chair. The chair tipped over backward with me, and I lay in the deepening puddle with the basketball floating by my dazed head.

This was very annoying. As I stood and slogged away from the waterfall, I could feel the extraordinary chill of the unnaturally rapid evaporation. The vapors were pouring upward from my body, and these vapors were drawn back toward the glimmering waterfall like some reclaimed essence.

I could no longer see the light bulb, so thick was the water, but the light was still on, causing the falls to gleam and sparkle wondrously. The gleaming beauty of it and the hazy swirls of mist rising up from the floor were terribly thrilling, though I was becoming so greatly chilled it was hard to appreciate the vision.

I slogged to a light switch and turned it off. The light dimmed only a little. The surrounding basement became darker, but the water itself was glistening gorgeously with interwoven flashes of cobalt and emerald hue.

Rubbing my chilly arms, with teeth chattering, I stood directly in front of the waterfall. Then I extended my arm directly in front of me to reach into the water.

Something grabbed me. In the next moment, I was drawn completely into the descending torrent!

Instantaneously I found myself in a moonlit grotto by a pool within what seemed to be a primeval forest of giant fronds, ferns and mosses dripping with moisture. Beside me was a jet-black waterfall with numerous little moonbows forming a ladder of colored light up the side of the cliff wall of the grotto. This waterfall was absolutely silent, and, but for the sound of my own heart beating, I might have thought myself completely deaf.

I stepped nearer the pool, and saw, on the far side of the water, a hunched presence I cannot describe. At first I thought it some Oceanic divinity carved from a huge block of teak. It was too dark to see clearly, but I had the sense of enormous shoulders and a monstrously wide face. A little bit of moonlight shone in its eyes, glinted off its teeth, proving something was certainly standing there more tangible than shadow within shadow.

Then I could hear its breathing, as though its breath

was the only sound in the universe. It seemed to me that a long arm was reaching toward me from the shadowy presence. I was still so extremely chilled that even my mind was working slowly, for only at that moment did I realize this was not a ghost, but the very kind of elemental I habitually avoided.

Where to turn and run, I had no idea. How to return to my own world? I stood petrified, and am certain that it intended to snatch me and throw me into the bottomless pit of that black, black pool!

Needless to say, it did not kill me, or I should not tell the tale today. But it was not due to anything of my doing. I gradually became aware of another presence standing a little to my side. He was a slender, black youth, smiling sweetly. He looked somehow heroic, so that his slim athletic presence reassured me somewhat. He was holding the orange basketball I had purchased earlier that day. He held it close to his chest, then shot it straight forward into the face of the shadowy thing across the pool.

I broke free of my momentary paralysis, which may after all have been imposed on me by the elemental. I turned to look the young man directly in the face. He was handsome with a high forehead, the most beautiful eyes imaginable, thick short hair, and a grin that captured both a sense of mischief and of sorrow.

I wanted to speak to him, but before I could open my mouth, he lifted both arms and shoved me backward into the grotto's narrow waterfall.

The basement was completely dry—and completely dark. I did not take the time to fumble for the light, but made my way directly toward the back exit door. The only thing on my mind just then was to get away from the elemental, even though it seemed now to have vanished utterly.

I got the door opened and stood bathed in dim light from all quarters of the nighted city. I was about to lock the door behind me when I remembered my book, the rather rare *The Bow Legged Ghost*. How could I abandon my book! I left the door open for a little light and took myself back into the gloom, not without trepidations, to fetch the decorative, ivory clothbound book atop the file cabinet.

As I took the book in my hand, I lingered a moment longer. With eyes closed, I could hear the good guardian bouncing his basketball far, far away, as from another dimension.

The Queen Mum

Anna Christopherine Bailey,
Portland, Oregon

Penelope Pettiweather,
Seattle, Washington

Dear Penolope,

I bet you're surprised to hear from me after so long. I'm a "Bailey" now, not a "Berman." Many of my old interests have fallen by the way—with only a twinge of regret.

You must understand, Penny, that not all of us with "the extra sense" have the stamina to always be investigating things. I married, gave birth to a handsome little brat, and my husband disapproves of "the ghostie habit" as you once called it in a letter to me. So little by little, I faded away from the inner circle of mystical delights.

Little things do still happen of course—it can't be stopped—but I no longer go out of my way. You'll say it's a great pity, a waste of talent. As for myself, I came to the conclusion long ago that there are two kinds of talents that just don't matter for a darn in our time. One of them is ghost-hunting. The other is writing poetry. No loss that I've given up both.

But something wholly unexpected happened to me recently. My husband (otherwise a dear fellow) doesn't want to hear of such things. So I thought I had just better drop you a few lines while the Brat is napping and the Master is away.

I don't know how to tell it really. It began so innocuously. As you know, we live practically inner city. I can walk over to Hawthorne and do all my shopping. I don't have to learn to drive, yet I don't have to feel isolated for not driving. I love the Hawthorne District; it's gotten increasingly eccentric. Book shops, coffeehouses, cafés, useless shops that sell chipped or worn-out geegaws they call antiques, and a pet shop with lizards in it. What else could anyone desire? If not for my baby-carriage, I could almost imagine myself a Bohemian once again. I know I've come to live too darned normal a life, but I do still like to be surrounded by all these artists and queer folks. Otherwise I'd feel like a ghost myself.

The downside is a growing share of homeless who apparently agree it's quite a nice neighborhood. I get to feeling so dreadfully guilty about my life, first for becoming a commonplace bean-head, and secondly for being pretty comfortable. There are a lot of people out there who aren't comfortable at all. I've allowed myself to become a "soft touch," especially with the homeless women. They're so *dirty*, and waste funds on cigarettes—yet I feel more anguish than annoyance when they panhandle me.

By now they "see me coming a mile away" so to speak, as I've taken to buying whole rolls of coins to keep with me when I go over to Hawthorne. I don't pride myself on it; I just haven't the foggiest notion what else to do beyond saying "yes" when asked for coins.

I do at least gain a few pointless adventures from my low-budget acts of charity. Once, at a month's end, when Jeff's paycheck hadn't quite lasted long enough, I simply didn't have any change for anyone. I felt so apologetic to the "regulars" that I inanely took a tampon out of my purse and gave *that* to a young homeless woman. You wouldn't believe how excited she got! It never before occurred to me how difficult it must be to get tampons if you live on the streets. Now she never asks me for change at all—just tampons!

But let me tell you, there is this one old lady, and I mean *old,* she's like something out of a horror movie. Oh, I know you, Penny, you're going to say I'm an ageist, that old people are good looking too, but jeez, there are limits. Imagine if you can the oldest woman you've ever seen, and not one who has aged very gracefully either. Now add about a thousand extra wrinkles and big folds of skin sagging down off her face, jowls like two stained paper sacks crinkled up and glued on her cheeks, and hair as thin and mangy as a flea-infested rat's. Add, as well, two big red cups under her eyes. I don't know what else to call them. Her lower eyelids have somehow sagged downward and become enormous cups that are always oozing thick yellowish tears. It's disgusting. And when she holds her hand out to me for some quarters, it's like a stick off an old dead tree being poked at you.

She wears big black shoes and layer upon layer of the most fantastic clothing—not just old clothes but *old* clothes, like she steals it all from vintage shops. They're not all that dirty, either, though certainly they haven't been ironed in a couple of decades.

To top all this off, she wears a banged up old tiara with some of the glass "diamonds" popped out. She says it's her crown, and fancies herself the Queen-mother of Oregon!

She takes good care of herself, I give her that. She smells like powder and cheap perfume with just a tinge of decay — awful enough, but nothing compared to the other beggars. At first I assumed she did have a home somewhere, or she wouldn't be able to keep herself so neat. I guessed she begged mainly because it's hard to make ends meet on social security, but at the end of a day, she had a reasonable place to sleep.

But after having talked to her several times, I caught on that she really was homeless. She says, "I used to have a nice house in Hillsboro, but I don't have it now."

The other street people honored her claim to being Queen-mother of Oregon, and called her Queen Mum, or Queen Mary. She told me her name was Mary Woods, and she was from Knoxville, Tennessee, but has lived in Oregon a good long while. At times she has this delusion that George Washington is still president. When corrected, it becomes President Taft.

I was out with the brat, pushing his carriage along Hawthorne, when Queen Mum shambled out from a dark doorway and got in the way. She bent down to play with Jeff Junior, poking at him with those five skinny sticks that pass for fingers. She ichy-cooed and wuzzy-wuzzied until Jeff managed to get his little stubby candy-stickied fingers in her hair to make a grab for the tiara. It was so knotted into her hair, Jeffy couldn't possibly get it off, but he could sure make her howl.

That's when the Queen Mum got a little wild. She clutched at her banged-up old tiara and staggered away, trying to shout. She couldn't shout very well, but she could make a pretty ugly noise trying. She told passersby that my son had tried to usurp her, that he was a pretender to the throne, but she was duly made Queen in 1908 and would never abdicate. It was a position for life, and no one would ever succeed in murdering her and taking away her crown.

Whew. I guess that tiara's the only important thing she has left, but knowing didn't make it easier for me. It was exceedingly embarrassing. I tried to just leave, but she followed along behind me, insistently complaining about my son's attempt to overthrow the queen. "Your little sonny will never be King! He can't kill me! They tried to bury me before, but I got up! I'm the Queenmother of Oregon, always will be! I'm older than the Constitution of the State! I *am* Oregon! Oregon is *me*! If you shoot me, sonny, you shoot the very earth you stand on! You'll fall in the black pit you shoot in the ground, and you won't get out, that's what you'll do, but you'll never get the Crown!"

It went on for quite some while, and was a lot more colorful than I can relate. She tossed her hands around like some kind of mad puppet, and her hair stood straight out on all sides. Jeez, I hated it. I hated that I'd ever given anyone of those damned beggars a single quarter if all it got me was chased back home by the ugliest old hag I'd ever seen in my life. It put me in a black, black mood, and as a result of it I was too frightened to go anywhere for two weeks after, for fear she'd chase after me again.

I had nightmares about her, too. In the longest one, she was in a big auditorium, together with the mayor, black-frocked ministers, businessmen, society matrons — all the leading lights of the city, with all their families, all of them dressed to the nines. They were making a great to-do over the Queen Mum. She was slightly less ugly in my dream than in real life, but that's not saying much. The whole affair looked like it was a lot of fun, but there was something in the *mood* of it that made it a nightmare. Every laughing face appeared to have a spider hiding under the tongue. Every shuffle of foot was accompanied by the rattle of dice inside their shoes. And the dream had a *stink* about it, of mustiness and mothballs and the Queen Mum's horrible perfume.

I was in a complete dither over her. I had fantasies of murdering her so that I could walk up Hawthorne and not feel threatened. But when I finally got myself up and out of my blues and worked up the nerve to do some needed shopping, I saw her again, and she didn't act especially strange (for her, at least). I don't think she remembered a thing about the event that had haunted me the last two weeks. She stuck her hideous mummy-hand at me, I gave her a quarter, and she toddled off muttering the Blessings of the Queen.

Now I must jump to the end, because only last week I was in the downtown library looking at some old newspapers. If you must know why, it was for Jeff Senior. His birthday is soon, and I have been secretly creating a calligraphied book that said everything that had happened in Oregon on his birthday for a hundred years.

One thing that happened on Jeff's birthday was a coronation. I sat gazing at the microfilm screen, reading this old article dated 1908, and I could hardly believe the coincidences. It said, among other things I'll leave out:

"Mrs. Mary Ramsey Lemons Woods of Knoxville Tennessee came to Oregon in 1853, and lives in Hillsboro. She was two years old when George Washington became president. This year, she turned one-hundred twenty years old. As the oldest woman in Oregon today, there was a celebration at Portland's Marquam Theater last night, and Mrs. Woods was duly crowned Queenmother of the state of Oregon."

And, I suppose, a good time was had by all.

There's one last thing I want to leave you with, Penny, and then I'll close. Despite some recurring sadness about living this ordinary life, as an ordinary mother of an ordinary child, with a more-than-ordinary husband, I really feel that this is what provides me with a lifesaving raft in a turbulent world. I find myself drawn more and more intensely to the Queen Mum. I give her offerings of sweet rolls as though she were a divinity. I buy her lunches and Jeff Junior is learning to say "Queen Mum" when he can't yet say Daddy. And I know, I just know, that the reason I feel such empathy for these homeless people is not out of any social concern, but because I'm too damned aware that not very far inside me, I'm a crazy bugger who will be a homeless beggar if I'm not careful. And I truly believe there walks this earth a woman born in the seventeen hundreds who is very close, now, to seeing the twenty-first century.

Your puzzled friend,
Anna-Chrissy

Jeremiah

"Je suis dégoûté de tout."
—René Crevel, 1935

My dear Jane,

I'm glad you received that copy of *Satan's Circus* by Lady Eleanor Smith. One frets about the overseas mail. You'll note that while the spine says the publisher is "Doran," the title page says "Bobbs Merrill," yet both purport to be the first edition. I'm told that Doran had a habit, in those days, of purchasing unbound sheets of other publishers' overruns and reissuing them under their own imprint. So you see, it isn't really the first edition except on the inside! I was also delighted by your perceptive comments on the outstanding story "Wittington's Cat." The compiler of *Giddy's Ghost Story Guide* completely misunderstood that one, didn't he?

Thank you for that perfect copy of *Stone-ground Ghost Stories*. I could never have afforded it over here. You'd pale at the American prices for old British books! The stories struck me as quaintly amusing rather than horrific, but there is a lot more to them than meets the eye, though once more the compiler of *Giddy's* failed to see much in them. There's so much to the central protagonist's character that could be further explored if some talented and enterprising fellow ever wished to add new episodes about the haunted vicar and his parish.

But, enough of mere fictional ghosts. I was chilled to the bone by your recent experience with those two paintings you were restoring. If you wrote that one up as a "fictional" adventure you could certainly sell it to one of the fantasy magazines. They needn't know it actually happened. But what a shame the paintings had ultimately to be covered up. Not that I blame you; still, I'd like to have seen the one of Death on my next trip abroad, and that won't be possible now that it's safely "preserved" under whitewash.

Did my colleague Mrs. Byrne-Hurliphant bother you *that* much on her English journey? She can be a pest, certainly. Please forgive my giving her your address. Now, at least, you'll know exactly what I'm on about!

Yes, yes, I did promise to tell you what happened over Christmas if you'd tell me that horrid adventure with the paintings "Gravedigger" and "Death." Well, a bargain is a bargain, so now I suppose I must. It's much more terrible than any of the little accounts I've sent to Cyril for his antiquarian journal. So brace yourself, and remember — you asked.

It was three weeks to Christmas. I planned holidays alone. All my friends would be off to other states to visit kin. And while Christmas is no big thing to me — growing up with both East European Jews and Southeast Asian Buddhists in one's motley family helps to weaken the impact of Christian holidays — it can yet be gloomy and sad when one's options are unexpectedly restricted. I can't count a couple of pre-Christmas parties I would probably attend. The fact that people are so fantastically tedious makes the *doing* something as depressing than the *not,* so you can see I was just in no mood for anything.

I'd finished some early grocery shopping and was coming up the backstairs out of a bleak afternoon rain, two bags squashed in my arms, when I heard the phone ringing. You just know when you hurry, things take longer. I dropped the keys. Then I tried the wrong key. Then I tried the right key upside down. By the time I'd tossed the torn bags and their content across the kitchen table and grabbed the receiver, all I heard was a faint "click." Surprising how discouraging that click can be at times.

But before I'd put all the groceries away, and pulled together the majority of the bulk beans I'd scattered, the phone rang again.

It was the feeblest voice I had ever heard.

"Miss Pettiweather?"

"Absolutely," I replied, affecting the prim and the resolute.

"I beg your pardon?" said the faint, elderly voice of a woman who must have been a hundred and fifty-eight if her age matched such a sad, rasping, tired timbre.

"Yes, this is Miss Pettiweather," I said, donning a more conservative aspect.

"I read your article in the Seattle *Times,*" said the cracked old voice. "The one about the haunted houses."

I winced. It hadn't been an article but an interview. And while the reporter tried her best to be straight-faced about it, it was so garbled and misquoted that even I had to wonder if the interviewee weren't a lunatic.

"Did you?" I said affably.

The feeble voice said, "If it happens to me again, I don't think I can make it."

It seemed she was on the verge of tears.

"What's happened?" I asked, worried that some wretched woman was truly in need of my special talents, but so old it would be difficult for her to communicate her problem. "Who am I speaking to?"

"Gretta Adamson," she said. "My heart isn't as good as it was. If he does it again, I'll die. I tried to tell the doctor but he said not to excite myself. He doesn't believe me. Do you believe me, Miss Pettiweather? Won't anyone believe me?"

"Oh I can believe just about anything; but I don't know anything about it as yet, Miss — Misses?"

"I'm widowed."

"Mrs. Adamson. You haven't told me…"

"It's Jeremiah," she said. "He comes back."

"Is it bad?" I asked. That was the simplest way I could put the question. And she answered even more simply.

"It's terrible."

Then very quietly, very sadly, she added:

"Every Christmas. But…but…" She broke down at that point and could barely finish: "He isn't the same."

She lived alone in a small, run-down house in a run-down part of the city. The house hadn't been repainted in a full generation, for even curls and flakes had long since come loose and disappeared, so that the whole gray structure looked as though it had never been painted at all. Most of the windows were cracked; some of the cracks were taped; and a few small panes had been replaced with wood or plastic.

The lawn was a miniature meadow for inner city fieldmice. A wooden fence set her small property apart from the surrounding houses and cheap low-rise apartment buildings. The fence was falling down in places. The front gate was held closed with a length of rope, which had been woven about in a curious manner, as though the inhabitant beyond had a secret method no one else could duplicate, thereby making it possible to tell whenever someone had tinkered with it. I retied the gate in a much simpler manner, then strode a broken stone walkway between the two halves of her little meadow of frozen, brittle grass.

When Mrs. Adamson opened the door, her white, creased face looked up at me from so far down, it made me feel like I was a giant. In her gaze was a world of pitiful hope, worry and despair. Her head was cocked completely on its side, resting on a shoulder in a spectacularly unnatural posture.

"I'm Miss Pettiweather," I said, hoping my ordinary demeanor and harmless, frumpy middle-agedness would be enough to reassure her. In such a neighborhood, it was no wonder she was leery of opening her own front door.

She was badly hunchbacked and the spinal deterioration caused her obvious pain. The smell of medicine assured me she had a doctor's care at least. Her neck was so badly twisted that her left ear was pressed against her shoulder and she could by no method straighten her head. But it was a kind soul inside that ruined body, and they were kind eyes that glared up at me.

I followed her into the dimly lit, grubby interior. Her shuffling gait was slow and awkward, as it was difficult to walk with such a horribly calcium-leached spinal column. For her own part, she seemed to count herself lucky to be able to walk, and bore up boldly.

She was eighty-five.

"Jeremiah died when I was seventy," she said in her familiar cracked voice. I sat with her at her kitchen table. "Fifteen years ago, Christmas eve, in Swedish Hospital."

"What did he die of?" I asked, moving my rickety chair closer to Mrs. Adamson, to better hear her thin, distant voice.

"He was old," she said.

"Yes, I know, but, well, it will help me to know more. Was he in his right mind? I'm sorry to be so blunt about it, Mrs. Adamson, but it's only a few days to Christmas. I assure you I *can* help, but I'll need as much information beforehand as you can give me. Was he able to think clearly until close to the end?"

"Lord, no," she said, her sideways head staring with the brightest, sharpest, bluest eyes. "He had Alzheimer's."

I sighed. I would have to grill her a bit more, to find out what Mr. Adamson's final days were like. But I could already guess, and later, after an interview at Swedish Hospital, I would be certain. The raving last moments, the delusions—in this case, the delusion that he had gotten into such a state because his wife had poisoned him. It was often the case with the more malignant spirits that they died in abject confusion, anger, and horror, hence they could not go on to a better existence elsewhere.

The tea kettle whistled and though I insisted I could make it myself, Mrs. Adamson obviously wished to entertain me. She got up, for all the agony of motion, and toddled weirdly round the vile kitchen. A moldy pork chop sat in hard grease in a rusty pan on the stove. A garbage bag was filled with tuna fish and Chef Boyardee spaghetti cans. Something totally beyond recognition reposed on a plate upon the counter, and, though it was days old, whatever it was appeared to have been nibbled on that very morning, whether by Mrs. Adamson or some rat I didn't want to speculate.

In some ways she was sharp as could be. In others, she was indubitably senile. I kept her company the long afternoon. She rambled on about all kinds of things, mostly pretty dull, but was so terribly lonesome I couldn't allow myself to leave. Fifteen years a widow! And all those years, she had spent Christmases alone in that crumbling house—every year awaiting…Jeremiah. The toughness of someone that frail is really surprising, though such stoicism had left its mark.

She was cheered no end that I promised to spend Christmas Eve with her. I think her relief wasn't entirely because I convinced her I could lay Jeremiah to rest. Fifteen years is a lot of Christmases spent alone. Such loneliness is hard to bear, even had there not been the terror of a ghost. So it seemed as though Mrs. Adamson was more interested in our Christmas Eve together than in the laying of a ghost. Indeed, she took for granted I could save her from the long-endured horror, and was more worried about the months or years she might have yet to live by whatever means available.

Later that evening, at home in my own warm bed, I was filled with sorrow to think of her. I fought back my tears as I pondered that wreck of a body, the years of desperation, the terrible thing she faced year in and year out, darkening her whole life. What will *our* last years be like, Jane? Who will come to visit us? Who will keep us company when we've lost even the skill to write our letters?

I was so involved with the pitifulness of her material situation, I was not preparing myself sufficiently for my encounter with Jeremiah. What could be worse than a sick old age, separated from the rest of the world? Well, Jane, something *can* be worse, as you and I have learned and relearned in our explorations. But I wasn't thinking so on the day I met old Gretta Adamson.

Her odd, sad sort of strength was the other thing that left me unprepared, and the simple way she took for granted that I would put an end to the horrors. She had looked so frail, and had endured so long, how could I have expected her particular demon to be a bad one? I wasn't ready, that's all, though I did do my research, and never imagined there were surprises waiting.

I visited Mrs. Adamson on two other occasions before the holiday in question, and reassured her about my research at the hospital where her husband died. She hadn't known the worst of his last hours, as she had been ill herself, and unable to be constantly at his side. The day he died, she had been with him only a short time in the morning, thus was spared the worst of his venomous accusations, hallucinations, and the screaming hatred that preluded his death-rattle.

I had talked to a head-nurse, who had been a night nurse at the beginning of her career fifteen years before; she gave me a vivid, startling account of Jeremiah Adamson's raging thirst for revenge against a wife he imagined to be his murderess. I certainly wasn't going to fill in Mrs. Adamson at this late date, and was therefore careful to avoid telling her too much of what I had discovered.

That that head-nurse remembered so much should have been a warning to me, as death is too common in hospitals for a nurse to recall one old man in detail. But I chalked it up to her youthfulness at the time — we all remember our first encounters with grotesque tragedy — and Jeremiah *had* been memorably inventive in his repellent promises, given his otherwise impaired faculties.

So I had learned all too well Jeremiah's state of mind in his last moments of senile dementia. Mrs. Adamson was able to tell me a bit more, and remembered other things piece by piece whenever I probed as gently as the situation allowed. But I couldn't delve far at a time, for some of it was too much for her to bear recalling, and much else, I presumed, was genuinely lost to her own age-related difficulties with memory.

"I would like to see Jeremiah's personal papers, whatever you may have," I asked a couple of days before Christmas Eve. Mrs. Adamson was aghast, for she herself had never interfered with his privacy, had never sorted through his personal letters and what-nots in the fifteen years since his death. This should have been another clue informing me that Jeremiah's tyranny began well before senility set in. But I continued to be blind. I thought only to convince Mrs. Adamson of what was essential.

"You see," I explained, "I have to find out more about him. You mustn't think of it as really being Jeremiah. It's only a shadow of him, and a shadow of his darkest mood at that. The afterlife mentality is very simple compared to life. It fixes on a few things. In his private papers, there may be some clue to the thing that he most feared, or most wanted, and whatever it is can become a tool to erase his lingering shade."

"He wouldn't like us to know those things about him," Mrs. Adamson insisted, protecting her husband with a peculiar devotion, and looking at me sadly with those sharp blue eyes in her sideways expression.

"Do you know the meaning of an exorcism, Mrs. Adamson?" She wasn't Catholic and wouldn't know much, but of course everyone knows a little. "There are many ways to lay a ghost, but exorcism is the cruelest. It is a real fight. It's a terrible thing for the exorcist and for the ghost. But there are other means. Sometimes you can reason with them, but it is like reasoning with a child, and you have to be careful. But think a minute, Mrs. Adamson, about the classic type of exorcism you may have heard about, with holy water and the cross of Jesus. To tell the truth, such a procedure is worthless unless the individual had some personal belief in these things while living. The cross of Jesus is a powerful amulet against the ghost of a Catholic. But if he wasn't mindful of holy things in life, then his ghost won't care about them either.

"But other things can become equally significant. Once I got rid of a ghost by showing it a rare postage stamp it had never been able to get when living. A pretty rotten spirit it was, too, but gentle as a lamb when it saw that postage stamp. And the ghost never showed up again.

"Only by careful research can I find out what that special item might be. The more personal the papers, Mrs. Adamson, the better it will be."

She sat like a collapsed rag doll in a big overstuffed chair, pondering all that I had told her, her bright eyes expressing what a dreadful decision I was forcing her to make. At length I helped her stand, reassuring her the whole while, and she led me to a musty closet in which we were able to dig out two shoeboxes held together with rubber-bands so old they had melted into the cardboard of the boxes.

Inside these shoeboxes were faded photographs and mementoes and yellowed letters and a lock of baby's hair in a red envelope labeled "Jeremiah."

"I recollect that," said Mrs. Adamson. "Jeremiah showed it to me. He had a lot of hair when he was a baby. Lost it all."

And her dry, horrible old voice managed a sweet laugh as she fumbled the envelope open and gazed at the little curl of hair tied with a piece of thread.

She told me, as best she could, who were the people in the family photos.

She became very silent on discovering, for the first time in her whole long life, that Jeremiah had once been unfaithful, the evidence being a love-letter written by her rival several years *after* Jeremiah married Gretta.

I patted her liver-spotted hand and assured her, "It is sometimes just this sort of thing that brings them back. He may have wanted to spare you knowing."

But that kind of haunting was rarely menacing, so I kept sorting through the two boxes. Jeremiah kept no diaries — it is usually women who do that, and they're the most easily laid as a result — and it didn't seem there were going to be many clues to the sort of thing it would take to lay Jeremiah come Christmas Eve.

In the bottom of the second box I found an old black and white photograph of the handsome young man and the strikingly good looking woman I'd learned were Gretta and Jeremiah when they were courting. What a smile he had! He wore a soldier's bloomers. Her hair was short and little curls hung out from under a flowered hat. Very modern, both of them, in their day. As I looked at this photograph a long time, the bent old woman beside me leaned to one side to see what I had, and she went misty-eyed at once.

In the photo, Gretta was holding a round Japanese fan. The camera had focused well enough that I could make out a floral design painted upon it.

"Jeremiah gave me that fan," she said. "I still have it."

And she rose painfully from the chair beside me and tottered back into her bedroom. She returned with the antique fan, dusty and faded from having been displayed in countless ways over countless years. To see that crooked old lady holding that fan, and to see the young beauty holding it in the photo in my hands, well, I cannot tell you how I felt. And she was so moony and oddly happy in her expression, I was once again convinced Jeremiah's ghost couldn't be all that bad, or she wouldn't still think of him tenderly.

"It was the day we were engaged, that picture was taken. He'd been to fight in Asia and for all we knew might fight somewhere else soon, and die. He gave me this fan and I've always kept it."

"It's our Cross of Jesus," I said, somehow overawed by the loving emanations from the woman as she held that fan.

"Do you think so?" she asked.

"Jeremiah died with the delusion that you wanted to hurt him, Gretta."

I told her this as unhurtingly as possible.

"That fan will remind him that such a delusion couldn't have been true."

I'd been doing this sort of thing a long time, Jane. I really thought I had it worked out.

On Christmas Eve I came early and brought a chicken casserole and a small gift. Gretta was overwhelmed and wept for joy. And we did not mention Jeremiah during our humble repast, for it would have put a pall upon our cross-generational friendship and Gretta's first holiday with anyone in many a long year.

She tittered pleasantly and made her usual horrible tea in dirty cups. The Christmas spirit was so much upon me that I actually drank the terrible stuff without worrying if her tea were infested with beetles. She opened the smartly wrapped present—nothing special, just an old Chinese snuff bottle that I'd had for years and been quite fond of. It had roses carved on two sides and it had seemed appropriate because we'd talked about roses a few days before.

Then to my surprise, Gretta came up with a box as well—wrapped in some quaint, faded, crinkled paper recycled from two decades before, and crookedly taped all over with yellowing, gooey, transparent tape.

In the box was a tiny ceramic doll that must have been fifty or sixty years old if it was a day, and far more valuable than the bottle I'd wrapped for Gretta. I raved about the beauty of the tiny doll, coddled it tenderly, and really didn't have to put on an act, I was honestly overwhelmed.

"It was my grandmother's," said Gretta, at which my jaw dropped open, realizing my guess of "fifty or sixty years" was off by a full century.

"You shouldn't part with it!" I exclaimed. "It must be terribly valuable."

"I won't need it any longer, Penelope. In fact, I haven't needed it for years. I almost couldn't find it for you. So you be pleased to take it and don't go thinking it's too much."

Our eyes held one another a long while. How ashamed I was of what I thought of that neck-bent, hunchbacked woman when first I laid eyes on her. Not that I ever thought ill. But it wasn't her humanity that struck me at the start. The things I had first noticed were her crippled pitifulness, her loneliness, her wretched old age, and the decades of accumulating dirt and clutter that surrounded her fading existence. Somewhere down the list of first impressions, I must have noted her own unique individuality, but it hadn't been the first thing.

And now, despite that she looked at me with her head fused to one side, with her face turned upward from her permanently crooked posture, I could see, how clearly I could see, that *this* was indeed the young beauty of that old photograph.

We sang carols out of tune and reminisced about our

childhood winters; we laughed and we bawled and had a grand day together. She remembered her youth with far greater clarity than she could recall her widowed years. Then long about nine-thirty, she was terribly worn out. Though she ordinarily didn't require a lot of sleep, this had been quite an exciting day. I could see she could barely keep her eyes open.

"Gretta," I said, "we've got to put you to bed. No, don't argue. If you're thinking of waiting up for Jeremiah, there's no need. I've got your fan right here, and with it I will lay him flat; you won't even have to be disturbed. When you wake up in the morning, I'll be there on your sofa, and we'll celebrate a peaceful Christmas day."

It was a half-hour more before I actually got her to bed, somewhat after ten. Though she insisted she would be wide awake if I needed her at midnight, she was snoring in homely fashion even before I closed her bedroom door.

I walked down the hall, passed the kitchen, and entered the dining room. I surveyed the room and began quietly to push Gretta's furniture against one wall. She had told me in one of our earlier interviews that Jeremiah would first appear at the living room window and make his way to the kitchen and thence to her bedroom. I went into the living room to move that furniture out of the way also. Such precautions were probably excessive, but I didn't want to stumble into anything if for some unforeseen reason I had to move quickly.

It was still some while to midnight, so I turned on Gretta's radio very quietly and listened to a program on change-ringing. The day had been tiring for me as well. Like Gretta, I thought I would be wide awake until midnight. But the next thing I knew, the radio station was signing off the air, and I was startled awake by a change in the house's atmosphere.

I was not immediately alert. The realization that it was suddenly midnight, coupled with a vague movement beyond the front room window, caused me to stand abruptly from where I'd sat napping. The sudden movement made my head swim. A black cloud swirled around me. The brittle old paper fan had fallen from my lap onto the floor. I bent to pick it up and nearly lost consciousness. I was forcing my mind to be more fully awake, slowly realizing my dizziness wasn't the natural cause of standing too quickly, but was imposed upon me by something *other*.

As I picked up the fan and moved toward the window, I was brought up short by Jeremiah's sudden appearance there. His black gums were bared, revealing a lack of teeth and reminding me of a lamprey. His eyes were fogged white, as though he were able to see only what he imagined and not what was. It was a very complete materialization and he might easily have been taken for a mad peeping tom. He raised both his hands, which were bony claws, and shoved them writhing toward the glass. I expected it to shatter, but instead, the specter vanished.

By the increasing chill, I knew he was in the house.

I hurried toward the kitchen, recovering my senses more than not, holding the paper fan before me. I was shaking frightfully, beginning to comprehend the depth of his malignancy.

There he was, in the kitchen, bent down, scrabbling wildly but noiselessly at the door under the sink. The cupboard opened under his insistence, and he tried to grasp a little faded blue carton, but his clawed hands only passed through it.

Then he stiffened and slowly stood, his back to me. He sensed my presence, and his very awareness gave me shivers. His shoulders stiffened and he began slowly to turn about. I took a strong posture and held the paper fan in front of me, so that it would be the first thing he saw.

He turned and, for a moment, was no longer a spidery old man. He was a young soldier, and he looked at me with sharp but unseeing eyes. I can only describe it thus, because, although his gaze fell directly on me and was no longer clouded white, he seemed to see something infinitely more pleasing to him than I could have been. I supposed he thought I was Gretta, and he was imposing upon my form his memory of her when she was as young as he himself now appeared to be.

He came forward with such a look of love and devotion that in spite of my persisting alarm, and due I'm sure to some occult influence rather than my own nature, I was momentarily terribly aroused. He reached outward to clasp his youthful hands at the sides of my shoulders. I held my ground, certain that my humane exorcism was having its intended effect.

When his ghostly fingers touched me, I felt a warming vibration, as though my whole upper body were encased in fine electrical wire, the voltage slowly increasing. The fan began to shine so brightly that I felt I risked blindness if I failed to close my eyes, but close them I could not.

Before my gaze, the young Jeremiah's angelic face grew sinister by rapid degrees. Simultaneously, the electricity that held me in anguished thrall became more painful. His perfect smile became twisted; his white teeth yellowed and grew long as his gums receded; and then there was only that toothless maw yelling at me without making a sound, dreadful threats I blessedly could not hear. The young soldier had withered and wizened; it was evil rather than years that aged him; and the claws that gripped my shoulders drew blood.

When he let go of me, the light of the fan went out, and I collapsed upon the floor, half sitting against the door jamb. Jeremiah loomed over me with menace, yet my rattled thoughts were pondering in a distant, withdrawn place. I wondered idly if the electrical shock had stopped my heart. I was dimly aware that my lips were wet with froth and drool, and for a moment I was concerned mainly with the nuisance if being unable to move my arm to wipe my mouth.

If these sorts of things were the usual result of my investigations, I should not be so in love with haunted places. I have occasionally felt real danger, but this was the first time I had been so insufficiently prepared that physical harm became inevitable.

His blackening claw grasped me anew and he dragged me across the kitchen floor. His other hand wound into my hair as he pushed my face under the sink, so that I saw before my eyes a thirty or forty year old package of poison—a brand from the days when it was still possible to purchase strychnine to kill rats or even wolves—a damp-stained blue package with skull and crossbones printed in black.

And I realized at that moment what it had to have been that I had overlooked: the critical information without which I was helpless before so malignant a spirit. *Gretta had indeed poisoned her husband,* out of love I do not doubt, and to end his awful suffering. It explained why, on that Christmas Eve fifteen years before, she had spent only a few minutes with him. There would have been no reason for the physicians to suspect such a thing; but Jeremiah had known, though he lacked the capacity to understand it as an act of mercy.

And now my face was shoved hard against the open package of poisonous salts. I clamped my eyes and mouth shut. Jeremiah's ghost was trying to kill me, and at that moment I felt he had a good chance at success.

Then a sad, raspy voice came from the kitchen doorway, saying, "Let her go, Jeremiah. It's me you want."

The calm resignation in her voice was heartbreaking.

The black claws let go of my arm and hair. I pushed myself away from under the sink. I was still smarting from the shock of Jeremiah's first touch. I could barely see, and when I tried to focus, it looked to me as though a young woman was moving toward me in a dressing gown. She reached across my shoulder and removed the strychnine from under the sink. A sweet, youthful voice said, "I guess I should have told you all of it, Penelope, but I thought you could stop him from coming without knowing everything. I'm sorry. Now it's left to me to finish, and there's only one thing that will give my poor Jeremiah peace."

"No, Gretta, no," I said, struggling to rise, reaching outward and trying to grab the package from her hand. But I fell back all but senseless, still gripped by the paralysis of the electric shock. I watched as from a dream as Gretta moved about the kitchen, heating water on the stove, calmly making herself a cup of tea, and heaping into it a spoon of strychnine as though it were sugar.

Standing beside her the whole while was the young soldier. She talked to him in loving terms, and addressed me from time to time as well. She thanked me for a lovely Christmas Eve while I strove uselessly to break the paralysis, tears streaming down my eyes.

Then Gretta and her soldier left the kitchen. I heard her footsteps, inexplicably spritely, echoing down the hall. I heard her shut her bedroom door.

And that, Jane, is the gist of a sad adventure. It was over. Oh, I had to suffer interviews with police and coroner. But it didn't take long, because, unfortunately, suicide is the commonest thing among the elderly. I was not pressed to tell the whole story, which they certainly would not have believed. As to myself, I suffered no ill after effects of the spiritual electrocution, which was, after all, less dangerous than actual electricity. In fact, if you will believe it, the next day I felt partially rejuvenated, and seem since that night to have gotten over my mild arthritis.

And now you may open the gift box I sent along, and which said on it not to open until after you read my letter. As you will see, it is Gretta's paper fan. I bought it at the estate sale, together with a few other small mementos of a brief friendship.

You will observe that the fan, for all its simplicity, is of the finest craftsmanship, completely handmade in a manner not seen in over half a century. When I first saw it, it was faded, dusty, and tattered to thinness as though occasionally sampled by moths. And the fan I've sent you *is* the same one, miraculously restored, as though cut and pasted recently, the classic floral design as bright as though painted yesterday.

I take this surprising restoration as evidence that Gretta is forgiven by Jeremiah and that they are now happily reunited — out there in the "somewhere" we're all destined one day and eternally to know.

Notes on the Stories

The Hounds of the Hearth
This was the very first story featuring Penelope Pettiweather. It was initially my intent to write at least a half dozen like it with the same unusual structure adding up to a book: tales beginning with a complete reconstruction of a supernatural event in third person, flowing into a letter written first-person by Penelope to fellow ghost-hunters about her investigations of the case. I began one more, about a huge green glass vintage fishing float that washed ashore on a Vancouver Island beach, with something horrible in it. But the structure proved a little harder to duplicate than I expected, and I could not finish the second one; if I ever do, it won't have Penelope in it.

Penelope became, instead, largely (not entirely) a figure through whom I could transpose "real" Northwest regional ghost stories and weird traditions, turning them into little pieces of fiction. There was none of that in "The Hounds of the Hearth" however, which really just wanted to play with the notion of an entire library of rare occult books being burnt entirely to ash, a thing I find far more horrifying than ghosts. Most of the rare books alluded to in the story exist, but a couple of them will prove to be phantoms if you put them on your wants list.

Serene Omen of Death in the Pike Place Market

Among the reports of ghosts in Seattle's downtown public market are articles by Seattle news columnist Rick Anderson: "Tall Tales and Rumor Put Some Spirit in the Pike Place Market" in the *Seattle Times*, July 12, 1983; "If the Spirit Moves You, Check Out Old Haunts at Pike Place Market" in the *Seattle Times*, October 31, 1984; "Ghost Stories: Early Enough to Get Scared" in the *Seattle Times*, October 26, 1986; and "It's Time to Conjure Up Tales of Ghosts and Goblins" in the *Seattle Times*, October 29, 1990. Many other reporters have written of this ghost over the decades.

The varied traditions are also dragged onto local afternoon talk shows for Halloween; I have done such guest appearances myself on just such shows. Once in the hallway headed for the sound stage I mentioned that I did not believe in ghosts. The producer stopped cold in her tracks, whirled about to face me, and said with horrified intonation, "Don't say that on the show!" They much prefer freaks and weirdos on such programs, not anyone rational. Even the science channel has to treat it as seriously possible that aliens from space built the pyramids; TV is not a good place to get an education. Well, I played along, there must be people all over the Northwest who think I really am some old time psychical research hobbyist who finds ghosts in every leaf blowing in the wind.

Additional elements of old traditions are added to my Pike Place Market tale, from my own discussions with people when I worked therein. The whole is fictionalized, but may be compared with Anderson's reports for the traditional elements. As for how these stories get started, I saw the origins of one of them. A store owner in the market became weary of seeing all the free publicity for the preposterous ghost story associated with a business down the hallway in the underground levels of the market. So she began telling anyone who'd listen about the ghost she kept seeing in the aisles amidst her stock, and frequently called out to me up front to attest to the truthfulness of her raconteur inventions. She never went so far as the bead shop that invited a Native American shaman to exorcise the place, complete with news crews present. The ghost returned in time for the next round of Halloween free advertising.

The Spirit Shaman
This story is considerably elaborated and retold from the traditional tale reported by William Arnold in an article for the *Post-Intelligencer,* October 31, 1979, and reprinted in Carol J. Lind's self-published *Western Gothic* (1983). The haunted Glen Acres Golf Course is today called Glendale Country Club. The club prepared a leaflet to hand out about their resident ghost, keeping the tradition alive. The few duffers with whom I spoke are of the belief that no one has actually seen the ghost in a great many years — unless they had first gotten good and snockered in the clubhouse.

The Forest in the Lake
Various legends of sea monsters have been written about in Ella E. Clark's *Indian Legends of the Pacific Northwest* (Berkeley and Los Angeles: University of California Press, 1953); Clarence B. Bagley's *Indian Myths of the Northwest* (Seattle: Lowman & Hanford, 1930); "Luhr

Lore" in the *Newsletter of the Nisqually Nature Center* (Summer 1990); "Nusqually Mythology" in the *Overland Monthly,* volume 32, 1898; David M. Buerge's "Sacred Burien" in the Seattle *Weekly,* January 1989; and a vast number more of such articles.

This "octopus tales" of the opening part of the story are obviously entirely true, the giant octopi in Puget Sound being the largest in the world and quite endearing creatures. The vignettes of their behaviors were taken from my own experiences, and did not need embellishment. The second half is just as obviously fabular, but only in its treatment of the octopus-like lake monster. The underwater forest itself is attested to by Northwest divers. My father, who had been a Navy diver in the war, remained with my uncle professional divers up until the 1970s. They explored the underwater forest; it is from them that I have taken the descriptions.

The Oval Dragon
A version of this Victorian fishermen's legend of the Point Defiance sea monster was reprinted on August 14, 1970, in the *Tacoma News Tribune,* and found its way from there into Carol J. Lind's charming self-published book, *Western Gothic.* Sea serpent legends, and especially lake serpents, are encountered throughout the Northwest (as in most other regions that have noteworthy lakes, bays, or coves), but the description of the Oval Serpent is unique among such lore. Whether one is inclined to believe in monsters of the sea or not, the story has nonetheless proved its sturdiness as a doozy of a Northwest traditional tale.

The Woman Who Turned to Soap
The main facts of this remarkable incident are told by Ellia E. Conklin in "The Lady of the Lake: Tale of the Corpse Turned to Soap Keeps Lake Crescent Bubbling with Intrigue" in the *Seattle Post-Intelligencer* (October 30, 1990). Conklin drew in part from a florid account written in 1942 by "a bulldog detective," Hollis B. Fultz, for *True Detective* as "The Corpse that Came Back." The most signal historic document is *The State of Washington v. Monty J. Illingworth; Case No. 1075* (Clallam County Superior Court, 1942).

The story is repeated as "Clever DA Solves Mystery" in Marge Davenport's *Fabulous Folks of the Old Northwest* (1986); by Mavis Amundson in *The Lady of the Lake* (Western Gull Publishing and Peninsula Daily News, 2000); and in Lynn Bragg's *Washington Myths and Legends: The True Stories Behind History's Mysteries* (2015). In 1997 I adapted the actualities of the murder mystery as an adventure for Penelope Pettiweather. It was afterward adapted as a stage play "The Woman Who Turned to Soap" by William Shephard, performed only once at Palouse Performance Project at Langston Hughes Cultural Arts Center in March of 1997.

Legend of the White Eagle Saloon
The conversations in this story are invented reconstructions from my own imagination and do not represent the people for whom they were named. The main incidents, however, are vouchsafed by the real Chuck Hughes and Anne Audrey. Their story came to me in the form of an otherwise undated clipping from a May 1992 issue of *The Oregoneon*, the article called

"Shots in the Dark" by Kristian Foden-Vencil. Penelope's experiences in the upstairs room are added.

The White Eagle Saloon remains an active nightspot for locals and tourists to North Portland, still as famous as ever for tunnels through which drunken sailors were shanghaied, ghostly residents, "ladies of the night," loud music, and tequila-drinking competitions.

Sarah, the Ghost of Georgetown Castle

Times reporter Rick Anderson has written that as many as three-dozen people claimed to have seen the Georgetown Castle ghost, but his was a low estimate. She has been the subject of an afternoon television program; I've heard people discuss her on local radio talk shows; and Paul Andrews wrote at length in *Parade Magazine* about the surprising experiences of Ray McWade and Petter Petterson while they were living in the Castle. Ray and Petter have been fictionalized as Jay and Pat, but the incidents per se are authentic and unchanged.

Fritz, the Gentle Ghost of Shaw Island

The tale of Fritz is derived from Don Towksbury's article, "Ghost House? Not Seeing Is Believing" in the Seattle *Post-Intelligencer*, January 19, 1987. My retelling conforms to the facts given in this case, with very little adornment. As an aside, the story of "Joan" alluded to as by Penelope's correspondent Jane Bradshaw, is a fine story by British writer Mary Ann Allen (pseudonym of M. R. James authority Rosemary Pardoe). It can be found in my Tor Books anthology *Tales by Moonlight* volume one, and collected in the Mary Ann Allen collection *The Angry Dead*. I have always hoped others than myself are charmed by the idea of two fictional ghost investigators, Penelope Pettiweather and Jane Bradshaw, corresponding with one another.

Ogopogo
Among the innumerable sources consulted for Ogopogo are these: "Kelowna" by E. Jervis Bloomfield in the Seattle *Times*, November 18, 1962; "Lake Okanagan Still Hides Slimy Ogopogo" in the *Daily Olympian*, July 25, 1977; "Okanagan's Loch Ness Monster" by Joel Connelly in the Seattle *Post Intiligencer*, July 24, 1977; and "The Elusive Ogopogo" in Carol J. Lind's *Western Gothic* (1983).

There are endless other references to the beast of Okanagan Lake, British Colombia, besides coverage on the National Geographic Channel's foolish series *Is It Real?* in 2005; the documentary series *In Search Of...* in 1978; and numerous other pseudo-science promoting TV series. There are many photographs that captured Ogopogo most unconvincingly, and several incidents of hoaxers who left witnesses convinced forever after they'd really seen it. The family movie *Mee-Shee: The Water Giant* (2005) was based on the legend of Ogopogo.

Harmless Ghosts
The events of this story are derived from my own family history. My Buddhist step-mother Lek experienced the ghostly haunting in our Freemont neighborhood apartment in Seattle, and my father investigated the possibilities at my step-mom's insistence, making the very discoveries recounted in the fictionalized version.

I sometimes think I should have kept the characters of my mom and dad in the story, as they were unique and delightful people, eccentrics I suppose, more so than Penelope and her friend. But they were alive when I wrote it and might have taken exception to any such portraits. Another story of mine, however, "Lincoy's Journey" that can be found in my collection *A Silver Thread of Madness* (Ace Books, 1989) and elsewhere, is a nearly verbatim account of an event from Lek's childhood that colored the direction of her whole life and made her an authentic legend in Southeast Asia.

It may surprise any who don't know me that I do not believe in ghosts, not a bit. Nor in gods, fairies, unicorns, Santa Claus, or Barsoom. I enjoy such things as literature. But I do believe my step-mom was one of the most honest people on the planet, not prone to hysterics or confabulations, and what she believes happens she definitely experienced somehow. That these events happened to her and she was not the least bit happy about any of it certainly does give me pause and wonder, as the two seeming truths—Lek wasn't crazy or a liar, and ghosts don't exist—are difficult to harmonize.

The Burnley School Ghost
The ghost of Burnley Art Academy was the most famous Seattle ghost up until the time of the Academy's closing. Those who have written about it include Don Duncan, whose article "Sleuth to Study Burnley Ghost" was in the *Seattle Times*, November 30, 1965, covering Susy Smith's arrival in Seattle and her investigation of the famed spirit, which resulted in a chapter in her bestselling *Prominent American Ghosts* (1967). There have

been many other newspaper reports over the years, among the later ones George Foster's "It's a Friendly Ghost, So f-f-far," from the *Post-Intelligencer*, July 17, 1981 and Kathryn Robinson's excellent article "Seattle Spirits" in the *Seattle Weekly*, October 1987.

My version, presented through the character of Penelope Pettiweather, follows the facts of the case very closely, and adds new material of my own investigation at the dental clinic taking up the main floor of the building in the 1990s. It was another cause to "pause for wonder" that no one in the clinic had ever heard of the old ghostly tradition associated with their building, but they all went ghastly pale at my inquiries because they were all scared of the haunted place.

Previous investigators did not report the phantom waterfall, which seems to be a new phenomenon at the site, devoutly attested by dental workers, furtively since their boss demanded they not to spread any tales of their experiences for fear of frightening away patients.

The completely "fictional" part of the story does not really begin until Penelope actually stays alone in the basement. Although I *was* offered the opportunity to stay in the basement, permission was withdrawn out of the dentist's fear of scaring away patients if they caught wind of ghostly investigations. I was left to imagine what would have happened to resolve the enigma of the ghost and the water elemental.

The Queen Mum

Mrs. Mary Woods was a real Portland resident. She purportedly died a few months shy of 121 years of age. But one does wonder if she weren't much older. I learned of her from an undated KXAS Radio script, delivered on the air in the 1950s by Northwest novelist and historian Nard Jones, and preserved by Pacific National Bank in a series of the published scripts called *Northwest Narratives*. Many of the *Epistles* tell rather "light" stories and this one is likely on the light side as well, though a favorite of mine; I just like everything about the tale. As for the entirely fictive Anna-Chrissy — after reading her letter to Penelope, I rather worry about her state of mental health.

Jeremiah
This scariest of the Penelope Pettiweather stories is entirely my invention, except that the scariest part, Alzheimer's syndrome, is all too real. The story was originally published in a limited edition pamphlet along with two other of Penelope's adventures, in *Harmless Ghosts* (Runcorn, England: The Haunted Library, 1990) which was instantly out of print. The Jane Bradshaw story alluded to, "The Gravedigger and Death," can be found in my Tor Books anthology *Tales by Moonlight* volume two, and collected in Mary Ann Allen's *The Angry Dead*.

Published by The Alchemy Press

Rumours of the Marvellous by Peter Atkins
Doors to Elsewhere by Mike Barrett
Evocations by James Brogden
Give Me These Moments Back by Mike Chinn
The Paladin Mandates by Mike Chinn
Nick Nightmare Investigates by Adrian Cole
Leinster Gardens and Other Subtleties by Jan Edwards
Shadows of Light and Dark by Jo Fletcher
Merry-Go-Round and Other Words by Bryn Fortey
Tell No Lies by John Grant
Touchstones by John Howard
Monsters by Paul Kane
Something Remains by Joel Lane and Friends
Where the Bodies are Buried by Kim Newman
Music From the Fifth Planet by Anne Nicholls
Music in the Bone by Marion Pitman
Invent-10n by Rod Rees
Dead Water and Other Weird Tales by David A. Sutton
The Private Life of Elder Things by Adrian Tchaikovsky, Adam Gauntlett and Keris McDonald

Visit www.alchemypress.co.uk
for further details of these and our anthologies

Lightning Source UK Ltd.
Milton Keynes UK
UKHW010244241220
375731UK00003B/947